Married by Treachery

BARBARA KLOSS

Married by Treachery

Edited by Laura Josephsen
Cover Design by @coverdungeonrabbit

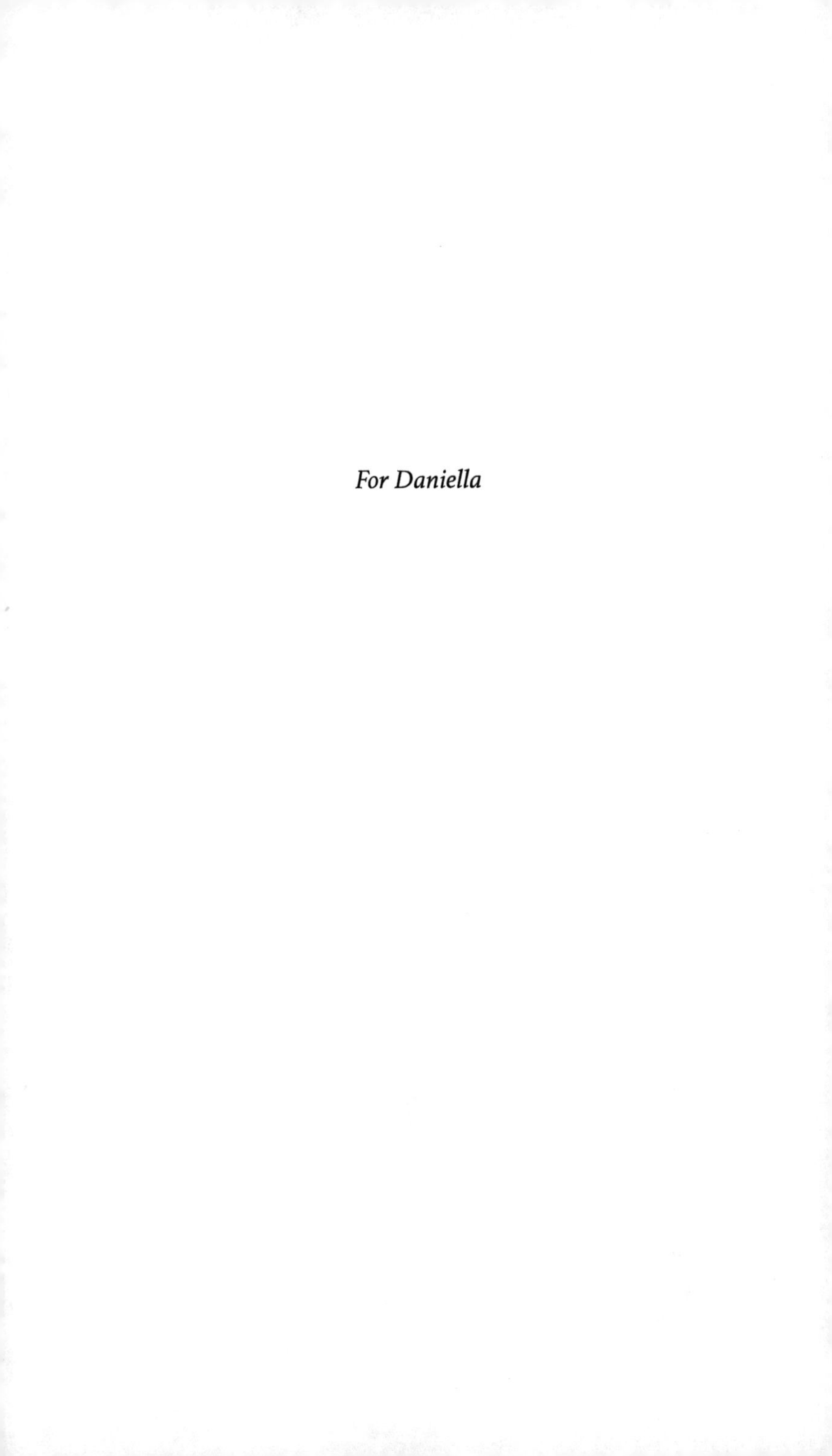

For Daniella

PROLOGUE

Deep in the woods, there stood a palace, and at this palace lived a little family: a father, a mother, and their two children. Twins, both sons. Most would call them wealthy, for their palace was second to none in grandeur, and they reigned over a kingdom rife with glittering lakes and magnificent forests, and they counted more gold to their name than they could ever hope to spend. But they did not understand—as very few understand—that it is not *things* that give one wealth.

It is love and the relationships rooted within it.

But this, they did not own. Rather, they possessed a perversion of it: pride, the love of *self*.

And *that* they had in abundance.

No one loved them better than they loved themselves; no worship was proficient. The more they acquired, the more they wanted—needed—to fill the hole where love was designed to be.

A hole that *things* would never fill.

The more they thought of themselves, the less they thought of others, until what was previously considered cruel became just and even deserved as long as it preserved self—such was the deluded and dark path of pride.

And so one night, after the older son told the younger about how he'd gone into the mortal realm and stolen the land along the wide banks of the Viara River by slaughtering every one of its citizens—man, woman, and child—an old woman appeared before the palace gates.

A Fate, they would soon realize.

She gazed upon them with a face like wrinkled linen and eyes like small moons, but before either son had the chance to wonder, she spoke their future into existence. "Such is your pride, young princes of Canna, that you have made yourselves gods, and it has eaten away your hearts."

Before either son had the chance to wonder, she spoke their future into existence:

> "Through blood, by blood, may your sins be paid,
> Spent from a mortal heart, the heir must claim.
> A babe wrought by harvest's light,
> And virgin be, by immortal's sight,
> Who holds the only road to your salvation."

AND THAT WAS the day the mist came.

1

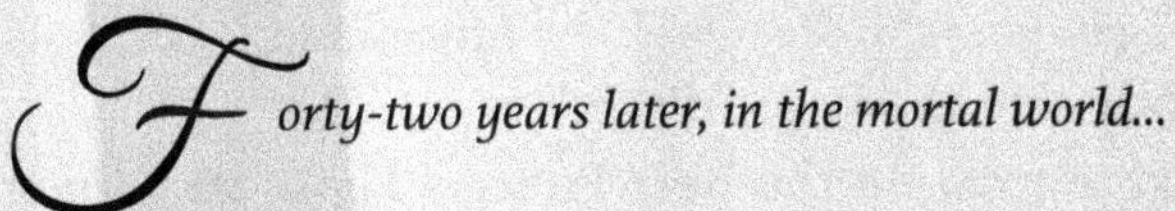

Forty-two years later, in the mortal world...

RAQUEL HAD NOT EXPECTED ALL the hair. The elders had mentioned Prince Edom's unusual hairiness, but this was nigh unsightly, and she would have felt sorry for the prince if he weren't also about to carry her off to her death.

Her betrothed rode into the village square, brooding mightily upon his enormous steed. He was flanked by a dozen of his kith, all equally brooding and magnificent, with their rich velvety green coats and gold-plated armor, reminding Raquel of brilliant harvest leaves. Of change and impending winter.

The townsfolk watched in silent apprehension as the Prince of the Forest passed into their mortal realm, their fear as palpable as the fog that had settled. Raquel might have been caught up in that fear herself had she not been so distracted by the fact that Prince Edom looked like...well, a bear.

She could hardly see his eyes through his mass of hair, which stuck out of his head like a lion's bushy mane. His beard had also completely taken over his face, neck, and probably all the other parts Raquel didn't wish to see.

Which she would, as his bride.

If she even survived that long.

Her older brother, Lee, elbowed her in the ribs and cast her a warning glance. "You're staring."

She tipped her head to him. "Honestly, you'd think the *prince* of the forest could afford a barber."

Lee gave her a very emphatic look, to which Raquel smirked. "I'm going to die soon. I might as well enjoy what little time I'm afforded."

"You're not going to die, Quel," he murmured.

"Six former brides beg to differ."

Lee's gaze fixed on the Bear Prince. "Those six former brides were not trained as you are." His gaze flickered back to her.

Behind them, their father, Laban, cleared his throat.

Raquel and Lee quieted as their father stepped around them and moved to intercept the royal procession.

"Remember what we discussed, and do not be too eager. Patience is your greatest ally here," Lee whispered in final warning, and then followed after their father.

Raquel sighed, gathered her skirts, and strode after them as more townsfolk slowly assembled to watch an exchange that many had witnessed before, seven years ago. And seven years before that, and so on and so forth. It was the only time that the People of the Forest could pass through the veil, and for *some* reason they always traveled to Harran to select a bride for their beloved (and hairy) Prince Edom. The oldest of Harran remembered the first bride from forty-two years ago.

Raquel marked the seventh.

It was an agreement between their peoples for reasons Raquel still did not understand. Of course, she understood those reasons on *Harran's* side: a mortal bride in exchange for immortal protection, and Harran had enjoyed that protection from neighboring kingdoms for as long as Raquel could remember. But what mortals had to offer the Forest kith of Canna, no one knew with any certainty. There was speculation, of course, but as far as Raquel was concerned, six young women had been taken from their village, and Prince Edom kept returning for more.

He'd offered no explanation except to say that if the people of Harran wanted to continue enjoying the Forest kith's protections, Harran would hand over what was owed.

Last time, it had been Lee's betrothed—a young woman Raquel had grown to love like a sister.

This time, it was Raquel.

To be fair, Raquel had begged Harran's elders to choose and send *her*. Without any vocal competition, save her own father—and Lee, until she'd explained her plan—the elders had unanimously agreed. Raquel vowed she would be the last, and Lee had aided her relentlessly with that vow.

"Prince Edom," declared Hamor, Harran's premier, as he and the four elders lay prostrate before the Bear Prince.

It was embarrassing, really.

The crowd followed suit, including Lee and her father, to Raquel's irritation, until Raquel alone remained standing.

The Bear Prince's dark gaze landed on her and narrowed to a blade's point. Raquel dropped to her knees but did not drop her gaze, not even as little pebbles bit into her kneecaps through her skirts.

Something sparked in the Bear Prince's eyes, and he drew his steed to an abrupt halt at the center of the square. His kith fanned out behind him, eyeing the crowd with the disdain of the elite. They looked entirely out of place amidst

Harran's dusty, sepia palette, these creatures from another world.

"You truly honor us this day, Your Grace," Hamor continued like any respectable sycophant. "It has been many years since last we—"

"I would take that which is owed." The Bear Prince cut him off. He had a deep and commanding voice. One that was used to being obeyed, and one that held little patience for those who did not obey.

The wind stirred through the pines, there was some shifting within the crowd, some covert glances as the people searched for the offering Hamor and the elders had chosen, and Raquel's father started to rise.

Raquel rose faster. "I am here, Highness."

The Bear Prince's gaze carved into her. Wind howled, but the Bear Prince did not move—did not seem affected by it, though it tugged strands of Raquel's long golden plait free and pulled them across her face.

And then the Bear Prince dismounted.

It was a swift motion, as imperious and sure as his voice, and his heavy black boots landed firmly upon the soft earth.

Raquel could have sworn the air shuddered.

The Bear Prince's gaze never left her face as he strode powerfully forward, a conqueror come to collect the spoils of victory. Wind made a maelstrom of his wild brown tresses, and his coat billowed behind him. He did not wear the rich greens and golds of his kith. His coat was the dark brown of his hair, the color of damp earth and tree bark. A visual rebellion to all class and decency.

The Bear Prince stopped one pace away, and Raquel forced herself not to shrink. Not to shrivel or cower, which was unusually difficult because up close, the Bear Prince was as large as any actual bear. He even smelled wild, and something feral burned in his dark eyes.

Those eyes raked over her body, head to toe. "*You*?" he said with sneering dissatisfaction.

Almighty as her witness, the only thing that stayed Raquel's tongue was the mission ahead of her. The one Lee had helped prepare her for.

Still, in her periphery, she saw Lee's hand twitch.

"The girl is Laban's only daughter," Hamor hastened to say. "A virgin at nearly one and twenty years of age, and she was born upon the harvest moon, as required."

Certainly there are other attributes to recommend me, Raquel thought bitterly, not realizing she'd muttered it out loud.

Someone coughed, but the Bear Prince's eyes gleamed.

"She's a good girl, Your Grace," Laban interceded, though his voice rang unsteady. "She's loyal and strong, and she will give you strong sons. If that is what you will."

The Bear Prince smiled. Or, at least, she imagined he did. It was difficult to tell through his thick and bushy beard. "*That*, I will." His tone was all mockery.

Raquel felt herself flush, but not with embarrassment.

The Bear Prince took a small step closer, reached out, and pinched her chin between thumb and forefinger. His grip was rough and firm as he jerked her face from side to side, inspecting it like her father inspected their foals.

"I hope Your Grace finds his bride acceptable," Raquel clipped, unable to help herself.

The Bear Prince stopped turning her face and gazed into her eyes instead. "That depends, daughter of Laban." He leaned closer, as if to share a secret. "How does my bride find her prince?"

There were words Raquel should have said. "Truthfully, it's hard to tell through all of my prince's hair."

Her father stilled, as did everyone else who had heard, and Lee dropped his head in defeat.

But, surprisingly, the Bear Prince tipped back his head and laughed. It was a great boom of sound that cracked the tense silence.

"The girl means no offense, Your Grace," Hamor stammered, glaring at Raquel. "Upon my word, she will honor our—"

"She will do perfectly." The Bear Prince waved his hand, spun on his heel, and strode for the magnificent steed that was less beast than he was. The next moment, a handful of his kith surrounded Raquel. A few seized her arms and began dragging her after the Bear Prince.

"But I haven't grabbed my things!" she cried out, and when they still did not release her, she added, "At least let me say goodbye!"

But the Bear Prince's kith only dragged her farther away.

Raquel looked desperately back, trying to steal one last glimpse of her brother and father, but they had been swallowed by the crowd. The Bear Prince's kith tossed her upon his steed, the Bear Prince clamped his arm around her waist, and they were off. Galloping through the trees and into the mist, away from the mortal world.

2

Raquel could not see anything through the mist except for the Bear Prince and his entourage. They might as well have been galloping through the clouds for all she could see, and a bitter cold pierced her to the marrow.

This must be the veil, she thought.

It was far more expansive than she'd expected. She'd thought it would be like passing through a doorway—a single step from one world and into another—but this was an endless haze of white and cold that only the Bear Prince seemed able to navigate.

"How do you know where you're going?" Raquel asked over her shoulder, but the Bear Prince did not answer. His grizzly expression fixed ahead, but on what, Raquel could only guess.

"*Do* you know where you're going?" she tried again.

Still, the Bear Prince gave no answer, and before Raquel could inquire further, the Bear Prince slowed their stallion to a halt, the mist thinned, and a great forest spread all around them.

Or what *had been* a great forest.

The trees were enormous, but they bent and twisted like old bones, their naked branches gnarled and knobby like arthritic fingers. Black and rotten bark sloughed from their trunks as though they were infected with some terrible skin disease, and the air smelled strongly of compost. Like sour earth and dying things. Even more startling was the color.

There was none.

Well, that wasn't completely true. It was more that everything appeared...dim. Raquel couldn't explain it any other way. It sort of reminded her of when she'd walked Harran's streets late, after spending long hours tending her father's horses. When the sun had dipped below the horizon but the night had not settled in completely and contrast gave shape to shades of gray.

Raquel had not expected this.

All her life, she'd been told that Canna—the kingdom of Forest kith—was unparalleled in its vibrance and glory, full of life and tingling with magik. All of which Raquel had believed, especially when one considered the unusual elegance of the Bear Prince's kith every time they'd ridden into Harran.

But this...this more resembled a scene from Raquel's nightmares, which she had aplenty.

Startled, and now a bit wary, she glanced back at the Bear Prince, who promptly dismounted. The mist seemed to curl around him, this wild prince of a dying forest, while his kith eyed the trees. The Bear Prince stalked forward and then crouched upon his haunches before a large tree root.

The root twisted and coiled like a fat serpent, as though bloated and swollen from its last meal. Raquel shifted in the saddle, straining to look ahead, to see around the Bear Prince's broad back, to see what he was doing, and he reached into his oversized earthy-brown coat and withdrew a curved dagger.

Raquel sat stone-still, eyeing that shining silver claw. This was it. This was the moment he would take her life.

Her heart pounded.

Yes, Lee had been right: she *had* trained for this moment. Extensively. However, "this moment" was supposed to happen within the confines of the Bear Prince's bedchamber. There was no way that she could overcome a Bear and two dozen armed Forest kith.

Raquel was determined, but she wasn't an idiot.

Mostly.

Raquel appraised her immediate surroundings. If only she could draw him away. Isolate him. Then she might have a chance. She was a good rider—better than most, thanks to her equestrian father. It didn't matter so much that she had no idea where she was, or where to go, as long as she lured the Bear Prince away from the others, and if she acted quickly—

The Bear Prince stabbed the silver claw into the root, and, to Raquel's shock and horror, bright red blood oozed out of it.

All of her strategizing promptly evaporated. "Is that *blood*?" Raquel asked.

The Forest kith cast her sideways glances, and horses shifted, but no one answered.

Raquel could not see the Bear Prince's face. He was still turned away from them as he observed the bleeding root and lifted the silver claw that now dripped crimson. It was a siren of color in this gray world.

And then he stood.

For a long moment, he didn't move. He simply stared ahead, as if waiting for something to materialize in the mist.

Finally, he turned around.

He looked very much like a bear in that moment. A bear standing at full height, one claw dripping with the blood of the victim he had just savagely maimed.

Raquel felt a rare spike of fear, and her hand twitched at her hip on reflex.

"Should we stop at Drava, or did you wish to"—one of the kith started, then glanced at her—"continue?"

The Bear Prince considered, and then his gaze settled upon Raquel. Particularly on her hand. Raquel couldn't be certain through all his hair, but he almost looked amused.

"We've no time for Drava," he answered in that same commanding voice as he pulled a cloth from his coat to wipe the blood from his silver claw. "But we should not linger, or Drava will become a necessity."

The Bear Prince shoved the claw back into his belt. The cloth, however, spontaneously combusted in his grip. He regarded it calmly—almost in boredom—as he watched it dissolve into ash and be stolen away by an errant breeze.

Raquel had never seen magik before. She'd heard mention of it from Hamor and her father and Lee, and she knew well that a supernatural force had protected their little village all these years, but that force had been invisible. She'd never seen such a tangible display, and it left her momentarily awestruck.

The Bear Prince caught her watching, Raquel looked abruptly away, and he strode straight for her and his steed.

But he did not mount.

Instead, he reached beneath her skirts.

On reflex, Raquel grabbed his arm and twisted, but he was *shockingly* faster. Within seconds, he'd trapped her arm, and her leg, and withdrawn the dagger she'd strapped high against her thigh. The one that Lee had fashioned for her.

Raquel would have felt violated if she weren't currently furious at being ousted.

The Bear Prince observed the dagger, then her. "And what, pray, would a fair maiden such as yourself be doing in possession of an item such as this? One *might* assume you intended your betrothed harm."

His voice dripped with condescension, and a few of his kith snickered.

Raquel's returning smile was mirthless. "One might also recall the abrupt manner in which this *fair maiden* was stripped from her family, hardly affording her any parting opportunities, like ridding herself of an item *such as this*. A hasty oversight on your part, I'm sure."

Tension charged the quiet, and one of the Bear Prince's kith sidled closer, clearly not appreciating the tone she had taken with his prince.

In a lightning-quick motion, the Bear Prince had Lee's dagger at her throat.

Raquel stiffened, head raised and neck stretched, all of her senses focused on the cold metal edge pressed to her skin.

The Bear Prince's eyes narrowed. "Your other leg."

Raquel ground her teeth.

He leaned closer. "If you did not wish for them to be found, my bride, you should not have fastened them where they would snag upon your skirts. A hasty oversight on your part, I am sure."

Raquel's cheeks burned hot.

"Well? Do not make me wait, mortal, or I shall scandalize you further." Mischief danced in his eyes. "Or perhaps that is what my bride prefers..."

A few of his kith chuckled at this.

Raquel fumed, still glaring at him as she lifted her skirts

to withdraw the dagger she'd strapped to her other leg. One kith cleared his throat, but the Bear Prince's eyes remained fixed on hers. Even as she begrudgingly set the second dagger into his massive paw.

"*And* your boot."

At this, Raquel gasped, now feeling truly scandalized, but before she could do a thing about the blade in her sole, a piercing cry echoed through the forest. It sounded like a great bird, but there had been an eerie quality to it that made the hairs on the back of her neck stand on end.

Because it had sounded marginally *human*.

Suddenly, the Bear Prince was grabbing her boot and pulling free the tiny blade she'd hidden in the heel. Before she could comment on this strange and irritating ability of his, he tucked the blade inside his coat alongside her other two, jumped onto the saddle behind her, and kicked their shared steed into a full gallop.

Thunder erupted as his kith followed behind at a pace Raquel was not comfortable with, especially in such low visibility.

On second thought, if they collided with a tree, perhaps it would solve a lot of her problems.

That strange screeching sounded again—closer this time—and she was suddenly grateful for the Bear Prince's haste, for whatever had *him* running was not something she felt particularly keen to engage.

"What is making that sound?" she asked.

Again, he gave no answer, but the mist grew thicker, the forest darker, and she could have sworn the branches were slowly twisting and reaching for them, like serpents. The Bear Prince muttered a word—a word she felt with her soul more than heard with her ears—and the mist around them thinned, and the branches stopped reaching.

That otherworldly screeching sounded again, farther away this time, and then they were galloping through the narrow gate of a tall palisade wall and into what appeared to be a large outpost.

Not a magnificent palace as Raquel had expected.

Even more curious was that the mist did not touch this place. This outpost appeared encapsulated within a dome of clear air. Within the wall, Raquel counted a handful of wooden structures, including a watchtower with armed Forest kith standing guard, while more Forest kith emerged from the lower structures to see who had arrived.

The Bear Prince slowed their steed and dismounted even before the horse halted completely, and a male Forest kith approached. This kith wore his soft brown hair long and woven into dozens of tiny braids, the subtle taper of his ears just visible, and his clothing looked as though it'd been fine once, a very long time ago.

The Bear Prince acknowledge him with a clipped, "Marix."

Marix bowed low before his prince, though not before glancing at Raquel with marked interest. "Your Grace. We were beginning to worry. The colony is moving north of—"

"We heard," the Bear Prince cut in sharply. "Did you not place the bark as I said?"

"We did, Your Grace; however, it does not seem to be having any effect on them. Not without you."

The Bear Prince glanced toward the gate, his thoughts far away, but then his focus sharply returned. "Hopefully you managed to ready my bride's bedchamber *without me...?*"

The reprimand was duly received, and a muscle twitched in Marix's face. "It is ready."

"And Abecka?"

A few of those standing nearby shifted on their feet, and Marix's gaze faltered. "She is not here, Your Grace."

Something dark moved within the Bear Prince's eyes. He took a step closer to his kith, who gathered himself as if to receive punishment. The Bear Prince completely dwarfed him. "What do you mean, she is not—" The Bear Prince glanced at Raquel and instead said, "Never mind. We will discuss this after you've escorted my *beloved* bride to her bedchamber, for the journey has surely exhausted her."

But Raquel had no interest in being left out of what would undoubtedly be a fascinating discussion, and she dismounted with gusto. "Oh, I assure you, the journey has left me quite invigorated. I could not possibly rest now." Seeing that the Bear Prince was entirely unmoved and bristling to object, she changed tactics, flashing him a coquettish smile as she took a small step closer to him. "And...if I am being perfectly honest, Your Grace, I find my betrothed wholly captivating, and I do not wish to be parted from His Highness for a single moment."

Truth be told, it had nauseated her to say those words, but she was here for a purpose, and she wasn't above feigning the simpering maiden if it helped her fulfill that purpose. And thus far, that simpering seemed to have a positive effect: no one moved to escort her away, and *every*one looked astonished.

Except the Bear Prince.

He stared at her as if he saw right through her little display, then grabbed her hand and held it firmly—almost painfully. A display of his own. Tit for tat. "And you shall have me," he said lowly. "Tonight, in our marriage bed. Until then, you will rest and save this...*delicious* vigor for the night."

He drew her fingertips to his beard and kissed them firmly, but not with any genuine affection. He was asserting his dominance. Rather than pull away from her, he slid his massive paw to one of the wide leather cuffs that she'd fastened around the end of her sleeves, flipped a clasp, and caught the needle-sized blade that dropped out of it. He winked at her as she gasped, and then he slid this, too, inside of his pocket as he turned and stalked away.

3

Raquel took inventory of her prison. It was a decent room, if she were being completely objective. The bed was full and soft and buried in thick woolen blankets, and the fur of an actual bear warmed the wooden floor. A fire burned in a stove, which kept the chill from settling deep, and dim daylight shone through the window opposite. In fact, she might never have guessed she was about to be led to the slaughter, but then again, neither did the pigs in her neighbor's pen.

After sifting through the furniture and finding proper places to hide the weapons the Bear Prince had not found, Raquel made her way to the window and peered outside. It was difficult to gauge time in this place. Daylight never drew to fullness, as if the sun hadn't crawled out of bed completely. Her view captured the very top of the watchtower, as well as two squat wooden structures and the dirt path squashed between them. A few Forest kith ambled, laughing merrily, while beyond, the mist swirled and churned like a cauldron, contained by forces Raquel could not see.

What a strange place this was! Not at all what she'd envisioned or what her people believed it to be. What would the elders think now, sending off brides to sate the prince of a rotting kingdom?

She recalled the speed with which the Bear Prince had disarmed her. Utterly humiliating and unacceptable! Lee was right: patience would be her greatest ally. Raquel inhaled deeply and wrung her hands. She and patience were not on the best of terms.

Light footsteps pattered just beyond her door and stopped. Raquel's heart pounded, expecting the Bear Prince, though logic suggested his footsteps were not so delicate, and while being near the Bear Prince was precisely the path toward her objective, she wasn't quite prepared to kill him *now*.

Planning and executing vengeance were two very different things.

Raquel inhaled deep, readying herself as she tiptoed across the room to the stand where she'd hidden the smallest blade. Her palms sweat as metal jangled and one of her six locks disengaged. Then another, and another, until all six had been unlocked, and she'd just slipped the dagger into her skirts when the door pushed in.

It was not the Bear Prince after all. It was an elegant woman with slightly pointed ears, and she carried a tray of nuts and fruits.

Raquel nearly sighed with relief.

The kith woman regarded her curiously with eyes like Harran's blue-tinged pines, then set the tray upon a table and started to go.

"When shall I expect my betrothed?" Raquel asked. Thankfully, her voice did not betray the nerves tangling inside of her.

"I will bring you to His Grace in the morning, and you will break fast with him."

Raquel could not hide her surprise. "*Morning*? But he said—"

"Those are his orders, my lady. Good evening."

"So am I to just stay—"

The woman shut the door, and one by one, each of her six locks clicked into place.

Raquel let out a puff of air and stared at the locks, feeling conflicted about this news. Tomorrow morning! She hated prolonging inevitabilities. Better to rip off the bandage and be done with it! Even more startling was that for all the Bear Prince's scandalizing comments, he didn't actually intend to share her bedchamber tonight.

Well.

Raquel pressed her fists to her hips. *Now* how was she to kill him? Her plan depended on him being alone with her, in their shared bedchamber, which should have been easy, given her position as his bride.

That was it. She would have to sneak into *his* bedchamber, no doubt about it. But where was he sleeping?

Raquel snatched a handful of walnuts off the tray, then moved back to the window, where she ate, watching the comings and goings of the Forest kith and searching for the Bear Prince while trying to make sense of this strange place.

Not that it mattered. She would probably be dead tomorrow, and the Forest kith would be left to suffer from whatever ailed them, but every future generation of Harran would finally be safe from Prince Edom's murderous—and hairy—clutches.

Still.

She hadn't expected to be thrown into an intriguing mystery right before death, and she never liked leaving things unresolved.

Round and round the questions rolled within her mind as the hours passed. Eventually, the guards upon the watchtower dwindled from five to three to two, the daylight faded completely, and all the windows within the outpost slowly winked out. It was then that Raquel finally spotted the Bear Prince, flanked by Marix and another who held a lantern to light their path. She sat up straight but ducked back so that she wasn't easily seen and watched them as they approached her building. They passed through a door, out of sight, and then deep and muffled voices echoed within.

Her heart picked up pace again.

Had the woman lied? Did the Bear Prince intend to share her bedchamber after all?

The building creaked and shifted around these three new occupants, and heavy tread stomped up the nearby stair. Raquel quickly blew out her lantern, lest they notice the slip of light beneath her door, and none too soon, either. The voices crescendoed just outside her door, where they abruptly dropped to whispers.

One of those voices belonged unmistakably to the Bear Prince.

Raquel didn't move. Her hand rested over her pocket, where she'd slipped the dagger, and she strained to make sense of the voices that had dropped too low for her hearing.

This was it, the moment Lee had trained her for—for seven long years. But no matter her preparation, Raquel's nerves hummed. Training allowed margin for failure. She would have one chance with this. She could not fail.

Her hand slipped into her pocket, and her sweaty fingers flexed around the blade's hilt. However, those heavy footsteps retreated down the hall and silenced completely.

Raquel let out a long breath.

There was a knock.

Raquel froze.

"Are you awake, my bride?" the Bear Prince's voice rumbled through the door.

Raquel's heart pounded anew, though she did not answer. Instead, she very carefully tiptoed to her bed, slipped into the covers, rolled onto her side, and slid her blade beneath her pillow.

Waiting.

But her door did not open.

Wood creaked as the Bear Prince stepped away, then opened and closed the door across the hall.

Quiet.

Raquel frowned, threw back her covers, and sat up. She hadn't expected him to knock, let alone ask if she was awake. He certainly hadn't bothered *asking* her anything since he'd taken her from Harran.

But her door did not open, and he did not come.

However.

He *had* given her an answer: the location of his bedchamber.

Raquel's lips curled. Perhaps this might work to her advantage after all.

She waited an hour more, just to be sure, then gathered the rest of her blades, tiptoed across the room, and bent over to study the locks.

All six of them.

She pulled two pins from a rib in her corset, smirking as she did, then pressed her ear to the door once more just to be sure. It took her all of five minutes to open all six locks, and then she slid her pins just beneath her neckline, careful not to stab anything delicate, placed her hand upon the door, and pushed slowly.

The corridor beyond lay empty.

A single lantern burned at the end of the hall, but her

gaze fastened on the door across from hers. The room Prince Edom had apparently taken.

Unguarded. Ripe for the taking.

Raquel licked her lips, cast one last glance toward the end of the hall, then gathered her skirts and tiptoed to Prince Edom's door.

She observed the lock, but instead of reaching for her pins, she tried the handle instead.

The door opened with the softest creak.

Either the Bear Prince was even more arrogant than she'd suspected, or he'd left the room without her hearing.

Or.

Perhaps—and she didn't really want to consider the implications—he'd fortified his room with magik she could not see. Whatever the reason, this was her chance. Possibly her *only* chance.

Raquel inhaled deep, pushed the door open just enough to slip inside, then closed it behind her.

So far, so good.

The room was definitely occupied. The sound of heavy breathing softened the silence, and sheets ruffled as someone turned. Raquel strained to look in the corner where the sound emanated, but she couldn't see anything in the darkness.

She crept forward, light on her toes, hands out and searching so that she didn't unwittingly bump into anything and forfeit her one advantage.

In three breaths, she'd reached the bedside.

She still could not see, though the shadows had differentiated into shapes. There was an unmistakable mass atop the bed; however, it didn't appear large enough to belong to the Bear Prince, or maybe he just didn't seem as large when he wasn't towering over her like a feral beast. Regardless, Raquel did not wish to die burdened with the knowledge that she'd murdered an innocent, and so she leaned closer to be sure.

An edge of cool metal pressed against her throat.

Raquel cursed inwardly.

"Now, is this how one treats one's betrothed?" asked the Bear Prince smoothly, his words lovingly incongruous with the situation.

Because she also had her blade at *his* throat, but now her heart was pounding. "You promised to come to my bedchamber," she replied, her words also contradictory to the vengeful fury in her voice. "I was beginning to worry."

A single breath passed between them. She thought she heard him chuckle, though the sound was too soft to be sure, and his blade still pressed to her neck as surely as her blade pressed to his.

"And here I was so certain I'd removed all of your sharp little claws," he continued in that space between them, wholly unconcerned. "Tell me, my *beloved* bride, where did you keep this?"

"You can't expect me to answer your question when you haven't answered a single one of mine."

He leaned a fraction closer, which inadvertently pressed her blade a little deeper. She still couldn't make out his face, but his warm breath brushed her nose, and his eyes glinted in the dark. "And what, pray, would my bride care to know?"

She almost asked. Her lips parted to start listing off all of the questions that'd been mounting inside of her since her abduction, but then she caught herself. "You're trying to distract me."

"Am I?"

She pressed that blade as hard as she dared, but the Bear Prince did not flinch, and also, she didn't feel any hair upon his neck. Adrenaline and circumstances had initially distracted her, but now that she thought on it, she realized her blade rested against smooth skin.

Confused, she reached for his face with her free hand, but *his* free hand lashed out with that impossible quickness and caught hers.

This hand also felt significantly *less* hairy than she recalled.

"It seems we are at an impasse, my bride," he said, as if the entire situation was completely under his control and it thoroughly amused him.

"We're only at an impasse if you believe that I am not prepared to die."

She felt him studying her.

"You are prepared to die?" he asked.

She did not like the mockery in his tone. "If it results in *your* death and an end to Harran's debt to your people, then yes."

At this, he jerked their joined hands around the back of her neck and pulled her close so that she was practically lying on top of him. Raquel strained in his grip, against the blade at her throat, their breaths mixed between them.

His smelled sweet, she noticed. Like the blooming buds of spring.

"You mortals and your pathetic ideals." In contrast to his breath, his tone held no sweetness at all. It was all winter and ice. "I've heard it a thousand times over, from a thousand different men, but each time your kind stares death in the face, you cower in fear. Every one of you. You do anything to avoid it. Betray your neighbor, your family. Because fear of dying is your greatest weakness and our greatest advantage over you."

Raquel trembled with seven years of rage. "That is true for some, but it is not true for me."

"Oh, and do you possess some rare power that evades the rest of your miserable kind?" he said derisively.

"I do, and so do others who are fortunate enough to find it," Raquel answered without hesitation.

For a moment, he did not seem to breathe. "And what *power* is that?"

"The power of love."

He graced her with a deriding chuckle.

"You mock it, but love is the greatest power of all," she persisted, conviction flying from her lips in passionate drops of spittle that (hopefully) landed upon his face. "It is greater than all the magik in the world, because love is boundless. It gives beyond all comprehension, stands beyond all reason, and it gives a strength of will that *your* miserable kind can only dream of, if you dream at all. But I'm not surprised you didn't factor this into your little equation, because your kind has no heart, and that is *your* greatest weakness and *our* greatest advantage over you."

One breath.

Two.

"You have given this an obscene amount of thought," he mused.

"Every day of my life for the last seven years."

"I might advise you find yourself a hobby."

"Lucky for you, I did."

Raquel had not been sitting idly while she'd been speaking. With the hand caught in his grasp, and in his momentary distraction listening to her speak, she had turned her wrist just enough, using his own grip to catch the small clasp at her wrist strap. As soon as she spoke that last word, she turned her wrist just so.

The small spring snapped, and the hidden blade stabbed into his palm.

The Bear Prince cursed in shock and in pain, his grip

loosening, but it was all Raquel needed to twist away from him. However, she'd hardly made it off of the bed when he grabbed a fistful of her skirts and yanked her right back.

She yelped in surprise, twisting on the rebound, and slashed with her blade. He ducked to avoid being skewered, then barreled into her stomach like a battering ram, sending them both stumbling back to where Raquel slammed against the wall. The blade flew from her hand as she struck the wall with impressive force, knocking something—a portrait? —free of its support, and it crashed to the floor as Raquel reached for his...

"Where is all your hair!?" Raquel exclaimed.

The Bear Prince grabbed her hands and slammed them over her head, against the wall, the both of them heaving. Well, that wasn't quite true. She was heaving with exertion, but his breath was perfectly and irritatingly even.

"And where are *your* manners, my bride?" he taunted.

"You speak of *manners* when you've murdered six innocent young women?" She tried to knee him in his Forestman parts, but he easily twisted away.

"Six innocent...Ah, you mean the other mortal girls."

"And you've already forgotten them!" She managed to rip a hand free and clap his ear.

He flinched back with a cry, which gave Raquel just enough space to slip out and under, away from him. However, he promptly grabbed her skirts and jerked her right back again.

"Blasted, useless heap of"—she started, and he pinned her to the wall—"fabric!"

To her annoyance, he'd fastened both of her wrists over her head with just one hand, using his body to keep her legs from flying at him while his free hand slipped beneath her neckline. She gasped in outrage. "Don't you dare—"

His fingers reached only so far as to snatch the little lockpicks she'd secured.

"Thief! How dare you! Return those at once!"

"Need I remind you that *you* are the one who snuck into my bedchamber in the middle of the night to murder me in my sleep." His one hand calmly gripped both of hers and held them fixed over her head while he held the lockpicks with his other.

"You left your door totally unguarded and unlocked," she shot back. "One might think you *wanted* me to murder you."

"I did wonder if you had the nerve," he admitted. "Though I failed to realize how many more little claws you'd hidden on your person." He leaned closer, and his sweet breath brushed over her face again. "I wonder... Should I strip you down until I've uncovered every one of them, my beloved bride?"

"Stop calling me that!" Raquel kicked high, knocked the lockpicks out of his grasp, and they flew across the room as she twisted away from him. This time she remembered to grab her skirts before *he* could, and she dove for the blade she'd lost. Still, he moved lightning-quick and was upon her a second later. She just managed to roll out from under him, onto her back, as she raised the blade.

Only to be blocked by his.

He'd pinned her again, but this time to the floor. His body was over hers, his heavy legs weighing hers down, while their blades crossed resolutely between them. "Most women would beg for me to call them *beloved*."

Raquel couldn't help it. She snorted.

"Well, that isn't very *loving*, my bride," he drawled, and—to Raquel's satisfaction—he now sounded marginally out of breath.

"I find it incomprehensible that *anyone* would pine for

the affections of a feral beast!" Raquel tried to buck him, twisting her legs to gain the advantage, but he remained one step ahead. As if he anticipated her movements and was simply toying with her. And while that was deeply concerning, there was something infinitely more pressing that Raquel needed to sort out.

"Where the devil is all your hair?" she demanded again.

His shoulders shook with quiet laughter, and then a light sprang into being.

4

At first, Raquel could not make sense of what she was seeing, because the light shone from a lantern *behind* the Bear Prince, and all she could make out was his looming silhouette. But it quickly became apparent that this silhouette possessed no bushy mane.

She might have thought he'd chopped it off, but it wasn't even the same texture. This was smooth and glossy, in contrast to that wild mass of tangles, and he'd tied it back at his crown, though a forelock slipped free as he leaned over her. No, he wasn't the Bear Prince at all. This man had hair black as night, a pair of intense honey-brown eyes that pierced right through to her soul, and smooth (*un*-hairy) skin. His features were sharp and fine like that of his kind, but mischief curled his full lips, unbalancing his aristocratic air, which Raquel found oddly and woefully endearing.

Saints above! This was not good. Not good at all.

And, to her dawning mortification, he was naked. Utterly and completely. Bare as a new babe in his mother's arms.

His mischievous curl deepened, and two dimples

appeared. It was definitely the sort of smile that *most women* would beg for.

"And how do you find your prince now that you can see through all of his hair?" he asked lowly. His words slipped around their crossed blades and grazed her lips.

Raquel's cheeks caught fire for entirely different reasons. She'd never seen a man naked before, not like this, let alone had one on top of her. "You could have warned me!"

"My sincerest apologies, my beloved," he said in that small space between them. His eyes were liquid gold. "The next time you attempt to stab me in my sleep, I'll request an intermission to clothe myself. However, I must admit: this appears to be proving a far more effective distraction than anything else I've..."

Raquel growled in frustration, shoved their blades aside, and slammed her head against his nose.

The Bear Prince, who resembled a bear no longer, cried out with a laugh—actually laughed!—as Raquel kicked him off of her and climbed to her feet.

"I think you broke my nose." He sounded almost impressed. He touched his nose where bright red blood trickled, and then he stood at full and glorious height.

Oh, sacred saints in heaven.

Raquel was definitely not gawking at him. He was going to kill her. One did not gawk at one's murderer, no matter how devastatingly beautiful he was.

"Get dressed!" she sort of shrieked at him.

He looked at her as if she were a crazed animal.

And then a light rapping sounded upon the door. "Everything all right in there, Jake?"

Raquel recognized the voice as belonging to the man with the braided locks—Marix—who'd met them at the gate when they'd first entered.

"*Jake*?" Raquel hissed at the Not-a-Bear Prince.

The Not-a-Bear Prince smiled viciously through blood-stained teeth. "Everything is perfectly fine, Marix. My *beloved* just wanted to"—those golden eyes danced—"get better acquainted."

Raquel made a face and those blasted dimples reappeared.

Marix chuckled from behind the door, and then his footsteps retreated. Meanwhile Jake, or whoever he was, touched his nose with his pointer finger, and both blood and break disappeared.

"That is totally unfair!" Raquel exclaimed as Jake crossed the room. "What are you doing?"

"Getting dressed." He stopped before a wooden chest, then glanced sideways at her and arched a brow. "Unless you've changed your mind...?"

Raquel scowled. He flashed her a wicked grin then turned back to the chest and lifted the lid. He pulled out a pair of breeches, a tunic, and some other item that didn't register because her attention had, unfortunately, drifted.

Raquel clenched her teeth and forced her gaze from his bare (and perfect) backside to his face. "What is going on?" she demanded. "Where is your hair, and why did that man call you Jake?"

He released the lid and let it drop with a loud thunk. "Who's to say I didn't cut my hair?"

"I'm not an idiot," she said, though he did not appear to agree with her. "It's not just the hair... you are a *completely* different man from the one who kidnapped me!"

He stepped into his pants.

Oh, mother of all that was holy!

"Mm. Are you so sure...?" He fastened his buckle.

What was she sure about? Raquel suddenly couldn't remember, and she squeezed her eyes shut so that she could think properly. "I mean to say that you *are* the same man who kidnapped me, but your appearance is vastly—"

"It was glamour."

She opened her eyes to see him holding up his tunic, appraising it. Taking his time while the lantern light warmed his muscled—

"Dress faster," she snapped.

He looked straight at her, his eyes molten in the lantern light. "I'm going to die soon. I might as well enjoy what little time I'm afforded."

Raquel's lips parted and closed. "You heard that."

He winked and pulled his tunic up and over his head.

Raquel had had quite enough. "*Who—are—you?*"

"Fair warning, my bride." He shoved his arms through his sleeves, and the inked vines encircling his biceps flexed and shifted. "The more you learn about me, the more difficult it will be for you to take my life. I believe it has to do with that heart of yours that you possess and I lack. It makes your kind prone to sympathy."

"Doubtful, in your case."

Jake stopped and glanced over at her with a thoughtful expression. "You are so resolved to despise me when I have done nothing but—"

"*Nothing*? You murdered my brother's betrothed!"

His features opened with an *ah*, and then he fastened the ties on his tunic. "The last bride, I imagine. What was her name again...? Adair... Adienne... Ad—"

"*Adina*!"

"That's right." He tugged on his sleeves and pushed back his hair, which had inadvertently fallen free of its tie.

"You don't even remember!"

"Slight girl with raven's hair and beady eyes?"

"She did *not* have beady eyes!"

"See? I remember." He glanced at the knife in her hands,

which now trembled with barely controlled rage. "Careful, my beloved, or you'll drop it."

"You wretched, heartless...*how can you be so callous*?"

He tapped two fingers to his chest. "No heart, remember? But to be fair, I am not one to get particularly attached. Especially when I know a person isn't going to be around for very long."

"*You are the reason she's gone*!"

He strode for the hearth and snapped his fingers. A fire sprang to life, and Raquel suddenly noticed the ampoule and silver goblet standing atop the fireside table. He snapped his fingers again, and a second goblet blinked into existence beside the first.

"If you think I am going to share a drink with Adina's murderer, then you have grossly underestimated me."

"I don't think I have." He picked up the ampoule and tipped it over one of the goblets, his back to her.

This was her chance. Answers be damned, she'd let this futile interrogation go on far too long already.

She threw the knife.

It was a good throw. Lee would have been proud. And the blade *would have* struck this abominable Forest kith right between his broad shoulders, but at the last second, he raised two fingers like an afterthought. The blade promptly flipped around and shot right back at Raquel, halting impossibly just one inch from her breast.

Raquel's breath lodged in her chest as she eyed that little flash of silver hovering in midair before her. She took a step back, but the blade followed. She stepped to the side, but still, it followed, never increasing the distance, while never decreasing it either.

Meanwhile, the man—Jake—lazily picked up his goblet and took a long sip.

"Scoundrel!" she snarled.

He raised his chalice in toast.

"Hateful...conceited...murdering piece of—"

"Here, have a drink." He picked up the second goblet and approached her as easily as one might approach a fluffy kitten.

Which only inflamed her anger. "You can burn in the fiery pits of hell!"

"I probably will someday, but before then, I would like to share a drink with my bride. And I find that awkward situations are better digested with wine. Probably a lot of it, in our case." He stopped before her, goblet extended.

She spat at him.

The glob of spittle landed on his chin, which he wiped upon his shoulder. "Yes, I can see why you're still a virgin."

"Ah!" She lunged for him—to what end, she couldn't say—but she did not make it far, because the knife still hovered over her chest, and the moment she leaned forward, its tip dug into the upper swell of her left breast, puckering the skin.

He eyed her. "I see this is a sensitive subject. Here." He held the goblet before her again.

Raquel clenched her teeth. "I *said* I will not share a drink with Adina's—"

"Murderer. Yes, I know." He leaned in close, over the dagger, his mouth at her ear. He smelled like the forest, like summer and fresh rain. "I did not murder your dear Adina, my bride," he whispered. His sweet breath tickled her ear, and a shiver swept over her skin. "She still lives. However, I would greatly appreciate it if you didn't tell anyone. Especially my brother."

Adina was...*alive*?

Raquel stood frozen in shock. Her gaze met his, and then she remembered how close he was standing, and she promptly looked ahead at nothing, though his presence filled her periphery and invaded all of her senses. "*Liar.*"

"I cannot lie, my bride."

Raquel had nearly forgotten this part about the Forest kith. She didn't know if nature prevented them from lying or if it was something to do with magik. Perhaps both. Whatever the reason, this inability to lie had made the Forest kith infamous for twisting truth.

"If Adina lives, then where is she?" Raquel asked.

He leaned back an inch, but he was still too close. "I do not know. As I said: I'm not in the habit of getting attached."

"Then how do you know she's alive?"

"She was when last I saw her."

"Which was *when*, exactly?" Raquel dared to look back at him, determined to find the lie in his truth.

He lifted his goblet to his lips and took a small, unconcerned sip. "Not long after my brother brought her into this cursed kingdom."

"Then she would've come home by now."

"So that my brother would realize I betrayed him?" he drawled, eyeing her over his goblet. "Come, I thought you were smarter than that."

An important detail clicked in Raquel's mind, which seemed to be working unusually slow at the moment. "Your brother is Prince Edom."

"There. I knew your little claws weren't the *only* thing sharp about you." He tipped his head and drained the rest of his goblet. "But yes; we're twins. According to the nursemaid, I came out holding fast to his heel, and I'm pleased to say I've been a proper thorn in it ever since."

Prince Edom—the *real* Prince Edom—was this Forest kith's twin brother. *Twins.*

Raquel was still trying to understand. "So you...glamoured yourself to look like your brother and came to Harran in his stead?" Jake gave her a very patronizing look, to which Raquel glowered. "Sorry, all you've explained to me is who you're *not*, so you are...?"

"Getting very tired of holding this goblet." He held the second goblet before her again. Seeing her unmoved, he sighed and raised his gaze to the ceiling. "My name is Jakobián Alistair Issacharvyzin Risorro Molto, second son of Issachar the third, and prince of the Court of Light." He looked directly at her again, and a grin shadowed his lips. "*Or* you may call me Jake."

Jake.

Prince Edom's twin (and slightly younger) brother. Raquel had never known Prince Edom even had a brother.

"You look nothing alike," Raquel said at last.

Jake snorted. "Thank gods."

And also... "Court of *Light*...?" Raquel gazed around and beyond him. "Your land is a nightmare."

"*Manners*, my bride," Jake reminded her, a glint in his eyes. "In case you didn't know, it's considered rude to insult someone's home."

"It's also considered rude to abduct someone."

Jake sighed. "See? This would have all gone over so much better with wine."

"My dagger is still pointed at my chest, in case you hadn't noticed."

Jake glanced down at the dagger almost as though he'd completely forgotten it was there, but then his gaze unfocused and slid from the dagger to her bosom, which heaved in a corset that suddenly felt very tight.

"Seeing as you're so concerned with *manners*, Jake, I thought you might like to know that where I come from, it's also considered rude to stare," Raquel said.

He blinked, the dagger dropped to the floor, and he met her gaze. "I was just wondering how in the Fates you managed to maneuver so deftly in *that.*" He gestured at her corset.

Raquel leaned closer in an attempt to be fearsome. "Just imagine how deftly I can maneuver with*out* it."

He raised both brows at that.

Raquel suddenly realized what she'd said. "That's not..." Her cheeks burned, and his lips curled like ribbon. "I didn't mean—"

"Here." He held the goblet before her once more and kicked the dagger across the room, far out of her reach.

This time, she relented, almost without thinking. As if her subconscious was trying to give her some other point of focus—some anchor to help her regain control of herself and the situation—but just as her fingertips grazed his, he pulled the goblet away.

"But you—!" she started.

"I need you to remove your wrist-strap first, my bride."

Raquel fumed and grumbled as she unclasped the strap and the little blade tucked within. She chucked the strap across the room, glaring at him as she did.

"*And* the one in your corset."

"Oh, for heaven's sake... *how do you know!*?"

But Jake only waited, golden eyes gleaming. She begrudgingly reached around and slipped a slender dagger from beneath the ties of her corset. This, she threw with so much vigor that it sank into the wall above his bed.

Jake eyed the still-vibrating hilt, then her. "I would so love to see you throw that with*out* your corset."

Raquel made a face, but he slipped the goblet into her hand and wrapped her fingers firmly around it. As he pulled away, Raquel asked, "How do I know this, too, isn't a disguise?" She gestured at his figure.

The corner of his lips quirked upward. "Would you be disappointed if it was?"

Raquel felt suddenly flushed. "My only disappointment is that I didn't skewer you to that bed..." Her words trailed as he took a small step in her space. His warmth and summery scent assaulted her again, and his lips twisted, as if he'd just counted yet another victory for some game he was playing.

"What are you doing?" Raquel demanded, but there was no gusto to her voice. Only breath and heat and unwieldy nerves, and those nerves hummed louder as Jake reached for her—no, *past* her—and plucked a brown coat from a coat rack, then held it between them.

It was a single piece of fabric that had been neatly cut and sewn, with wide sleeves, its hem and neck trimmed with embroidery. Those stitches had been made with golden thread—a gold that matched Jake's eyes, Raquel noted.

However.

"Why are you showing me this—blazing stars in heaven!" Raquel gasped.

Jake had opened the coat and pulled it around his shoulders. The effect had been both instantaneous and transformative, changing the man before her into the Bear Prince. He now towered over her, all boorishness and wild hair—he even smelled of sour earth again!—and those dark and feral eyes burned into her.

Raquel touched her fingers to her mouth and took an involuntary step back, marveling at the complete transformation. "How... how is this possible?"

"With rare and *very* powerful magik." He pulled it free, and in a blink, he was his (painfully charming) self again. "Though I've recently been told this kind of magik is nothing compared to your supreme mortal powers of *love*."

Raquel ignored the slight, instead wondering at the kind of magik that could make a man appear exactly like another, even down to the sensory details. "Are *you* the one who's been stealing our brides all these years?" Because if it had been Jake, it drastically altered her present objective.

"No, no," Jake answered, and he must have seen the skepticism written all over Raquel's face, because he added, "Upon my word, it has always been my brother, Edom, until now."

Raquel searched his (handsome) face. Did she believe him? Did she even have a choice? He was kith and physically incapable of lying, after all. So if it had truly been Edom all the previous years— "Then why now?"

That kith wildness reflected in his eyes, and he leaned a fraction closer. "Why, indeed?"

She glared at him, waiting for him to elaborate, but he didn't. Instead, he reached past her and returned the coat to its hook.

"What are you going to do with me?" she asked, trying again to get to the bottom of this.

But Jake only smiled wide, showing off a set of perfect white teeth. "I am going to marry you properly." And then he winked as he flicked her ear—she flinched—and strode for the hearth.

And Raquel wondered...

Would the coat transform her? Could she steal it and use it to escape? There was the issue of her voice. While the coat had made Jake appear like a totally different man, it had not changed his voice, and her soft tone—coming from that Bear Prince—would be alarming to anyone who heard it.

"Don't even think about it." Jake sat in the high-backed chair. "The glamour won't work for you. It's fashioned specifically for me."

Raquel pursed her lips and folded her arms. "So you can read minds too?"

"Just yours." He winked again and refilled his goblet. "Come. Sit." He nodded toward the chair opposite.

Well, this wasn't at all how she'd planned for the evening to go.

However.

Jake appeared to be willing to talk, and perhaps if she indulged him in this, he would answer some of her questions. Namely: who in the heavens deserved her vengeance now? If Adina still lived, what had happened to the other five brides? Why had Jake come this time, and what did he plan to do with her?

Besides, she couldn't run blindly into the mist, and while she was determined, she wasn't an idiot. If she was to escape and find a way to put an end to Harran's suffering, she needed an accurate picture of her circumstances.

In her deliberation, Jake added, "I won't bite." He flashed his teeth in jest, but something wild danced in his eyes.

Raquel was swiftly reminded that he was not human. He was *kith*. As dangerous as he was beautiful—and he *was* beautiful.

Jake arched a brow and leaned forward in his chair. "Unless you want me to, my bride."

"My *name* is Raquel," Raquel snapped. "And the only thing I want is for you to answer my questions."

Jake sat back in his chair and let his goblet dangle from his long fingers. "Careful what you wish for...*Raquel*." His gaze flickered to her, full of derision. "Answers don't always speak in a language we understand, and even when they do, they oftentimes reveal things we do not wish to know."

"I am willing to take my chances."

Jake sighed and dragged his goblet to his lips. "They always are," he murmured, and he took another sip.

Raquel wondered at that comment, but only briefly, and took a step forward, then another, until she found herself standing opposite Jake. His gaze lifted to hers, where it locked, following her every motion until she sat primly down in the chair opposite him.

"Relax," he said.

"I am relaxed."

"You're sitting like you've got a sword at your back." And then he pulled his goblet away and eyed her. "*Do* you have a sword at your back?"

"If I do, you're losing your touch."

His eyes gleamed all over her. "Unlikely."

"And anyway," she continued, ignoring the sudden warmth that filled her belly, "*you* abducted me from my home—"

"You offered yourself..."

"—and then you dragged me through a forest—"

"That was my horse, actually."

"You took all of my daggers—"

"Save the one you tried to murder me with a moment ago..."

"—*and* locked me in a room... How can you *possibly* expect me to relax?"

He frowned. "Do you find your bedchamber inadequate?"

"*Prison*," she amended.

"You call *that* a prison? Clearly, I have underestimated your upbringing—"

Raquel growled in frustration. "Would you just..." She'd raised a hand as if to throttle him or grasp hold of all the words that *had been* there a second ago, but then Jake gave her that infuriating smile again. "This is all just a game to you, isn't it?"

"Life is a game, my bride. One long, exhausting game. We win. We lose." He raised his goblet. "And we drink to endure it all."

Raquel regarded him flatly. "How inspiring."

"That is wisdom you mortals can never quite comprehend, given your meager little lifespans. You're welcome." He tipped his goblet toward her.

"Yes, well, not all of us are blessed with so many years to waste away, and we must make the most of the time afforded us."

"By dying."

His mockery and incessant disregard of Harran's suffering made something snap inside of her. "*We all die*. All the magik in the world won't save you or your kith from fate. Your years may be longer than ours, but they are numbered just the same. Life isn't a game, Jake. It isn't something to play at or *endure*. It is a *gift*, coveted by those who would give anything to still have breath in their lungs—breath you and your kith take for granted. *I don't have time* to take it for granted. Every second counts for me. And you... you have so much time and all the resources in the world, yet you whittle them away on drink and *games* that cause the rest of us pain and suffering."

Her words were met with a silence so profound that she could hear her own heart beating a strong and unsteady rhythm in her chest.

Jake's gaze sharpened and fixed immutably on hers, and the goblet stilled in his hands. "If I recall, your people have long benefited from mine." His tone was low and edged with something wild and dangerous.

Despite her better judgement, Raquel did not back down. "And we pay for that *benefit* in blood. What I want to know, *Your Grace*, is how you intend to use *mine*?"

Before Jake could answer, or murder her outright, a piercing shriek echoed through the night. It was the same sound she'd heard earlier when Jake and his company had escorted her through the mist and dead trees.

Jake shoved himself from the chair and reached the window in two strides.

Raquel stood. "What *is* that sound?"

There was a knock on the door, but it proved only a perfunctory warning. The door swung open, and a large Forest kith man stormed through. Raquel recognized him from her escort, though she didn't know his name.

He stopped just inside the door, where he bowed and cast Raquel a sideways glance. "Your Grace. Apologies for the interruption, but you are needed at the gate."

If Raquel had thought Jake dangerous before, he looked predatory now.

The man's expression faltered beneath Jake's lethal stare, and he added, quietly, "You know I wouldn't have interrupted if it weren't absolutely necessary, Your Grace."

"That is why I ordered five of you here," Jake said through his teeth. "So that *I* wouldn't be necessary."

The man lifted his gaze. "Five are not enough."

Jake stilled, and something passed between the men. That horrible shrieking sounded again, closer this time, then Jake cursed and strode for the door.

Raquel strode for the door too.

Jake spun on her. "*No.*" He was all fire and authority, and Raquel shrank back on pure instinct. "You will wait here until I say otherwise."

He continued after the other Forest kith man, who waited at the door.

"I am not a dog that you can order to sit and stay," Raquel said after him.

Jake stopped at the door and looked back at her, but there was nothing friendly in his gaze. "Correct. You are my bride, and I am your prince, and you will do exactly as I have commanded."

He ducked through the door.

"But you can't just—" Raquel ran after him, but the door slammed in her face. She reached for the handle, which suddenly glowed and burned fire-hot. She jerked her hand back on reflex, hissing in pain as that handle *melted* into the door and frame, trapping her behind it.

Raquel slammed her fists upon the door. "You conceited —heartless—Ah!"

But Jake was already gone.

5

Jake watched the metal leak into the door's joints, sealing Raquel behind it. He heard her fists slam against wood as she screamed, "You conceited—heartless—Ah!"

"Determined little thing," Rian murmured.

He had no idea.

"I'll admit," Rian continued. Jake could now hear Raquel pacing on the other side of the door. "I didn't believe Marix when he said the mortal was in your chambers. I thought you were *waiting*." Rian's last word baited.

"I am." Jake smiled. "She tried to slit my throat just now."

Rian blinked, clearly not expecting that response. "She...*what*?"

A vision of her face suddenly appeared in Jake's mind, cheeks blotched with indignation, blue eyes bright with fury, wisps of sun-gold hair floating defiantly about her face, and he grinned despite himself. But then that vision morphed, drifting to the picture of her full and heaving bosom bursting within that skin-tight corset.

In the distance, another shriek echoed, but Jake was so consumed by that vision of her that he hardly heard it.

"Uh… Jake?" Rian studied him.

Jake promptly turned from the door and his indignant bride and strode for the stair while Rian hurried to keep pace beside him. "So *why*, exactly, am I needed at the gate?"

Rian glanced behind them. "Should I send someone to guard her door?"

"I thought we were short on resources." Jake looked sideways at his man, who flinched at the reprimand. "Forget the girl," Jake continued, waving a dismissive hand in Raquel's general direction, and then they jogged down the stairs as another shriek echoed through the night. "There had better be a hundred of those bastards, or else you—"

"Closer to two hundred."

Jake stopped so abruptly at the bottom of the stairs that Rian nearly bumped into him. "*What*?"

Rian gave him an emphatic look. "Sienne's arrived—"

"Yes, I figured that much!"

Jake's cousin, Sienne, had professed loyalty to him, and she'd further proven it by her generous donation of twenty warriors, including two elite. She'd never cared for her uncle—Jake's father and Canna's king—and she liked Edom even less. So when Jake had divulged his intentions seven years ago, shortly after he failed to abduct the last bride, Sienne had not hesitated to join his cause. She had, however, hesitated with Jake's logistics. So many kith moving through the forest would certainly draw *them*.

Which was why Jake had ordered not one, not two—not even three—but *five* of his elite to stand over that gate. Well, four. Rian was currently beside him, and, as if the Fates themselves intervened to confirm Rian's claim, the night suddenly erupted in monstrous shrieking.

Jake punched through the door and into the night. Little

Mignon was wide awake, everyone bolting down the streets, in and out of doors, rushing for the gate where—

Jake's jaw dropped and a curse fell out of it. Above the gate, winged black shadows swarmed like hornets, trying to penetrate the invisible magik barrier that protected them within this little outpost. It was a barrier Jake had constructed himself, and he'd been quite proud of it too; however, as he watched those enormous swarming demons, he began to wonder if he'd overestimated his abilities. It was a rare occurrence, but it did happen.

"Where in hell did they all come from?" Jake said, aghast. Both he and Rian were now sprinting for the gate.

"No idea! But it's all we can do to keep them off Sienne, never mind open the gate..."

Jake's kith fought at the watchtower and along the wall's inner walkway, trying to hold back those Depraved that managed to reach through the barrier. Light flickered in the mist beyond the wall—undoubtedly Sienne and her warriors trying to clear a path so that they could open the gate without letting the Depraved flood Little Mignon.

But Fates have mercy, Jake had never seen so many Depraved at once.

It was getting worse. The curse was growing stronger.

Jake and Rian were almost to the gate when Rian yelled, "Jake, your sword!"

Jake cursed and skidded to a halt, and Rian stopped beside him. He couldn't believe he'd forgotten to grab Lightbringer! That wasn't like him at all. He'd been entirely distracted by that stubborn, idealistic, *beautiful*—

"Should we go back?" Rian asked.

Jake looked at the wall. More light flashed, Depraved shrieked, and Corval—one of Jake's warriors—screamed as his body was pulled from the wall and into the mist, where it disappeared.

Jake ripped one of Rian's swords from its sheath.

"Hey!" Rian exclaimed.

"You never use this one anyway!" Jake sprinted on and ripped another sword right from the hands of a guard.

"Give that back, you—!"

"Thanks, Aimes!" Jake called over his shoulder.

Aimes stopped, finally realizing who it was. "Happy to be of service, Your Grace!"

"Open the gate!" Jake yelled at Marix, who stood at the gears.

But Marix did not hear him. He was too busy hacking through the onslaught of Depraved, and Jake watched as another guard—Maribel—was plucked from the watch-tower, screaming as guards tried—and failed—to pull her back.

"MARIX! *OPEN THE DAMNED GATE*!"

Marix looked back then, sweating and dripping in black Depraved blood. He shoved his way to the lever and started pulling it himself. Metal groaned as the gate swung inward, and Jake slipped through, into the mist.

6

To say that Raquel was annoyed was an understatement. She paced before the glowing hearth in Jake's luxurious bedchamber while occasionally throwing what appeared to be precious artifacts against his welded door. How *dare* he order her around like a dog. Who did he think he was? The King of the Forest?

Raquel stopped pacing, shut her eyes, and clenched her teeth. Yes, well, so he practically was.

That arrogant, heartless, self-centered…

All of a sudden, horrific shrieks blared through the night. Voices yelled, and the air rattled with an explosion.

What in the world…?

Raquel glanced about the room for the…window. Where was it? It had been there a moment ago. Yes, she distinctly remembered Jake striding for it immediately after they'd first heard the shrieking, but there was no window now. The walls were long and blank and stained in soot…

Her eyes narrowed on the little brown cape hanging so innocently from its hook.

Glamour.

On a hunch, she strode to the far wall where she remembered the window. She pressed her palms to the wooden planks and their grooves, dragging her hands along the places she thought the window *should* be, until—ah! Her fingers rounded a lip of wood. She couldn't see it—no—not with her eyes, but she definitely traced the firm symmetrical edge of what was undoubtedly a large windowsill. She slid her hands to the center, and her palms grazed cool glass.

Her lips curled. "You tricky little prince." Perhaps if she could just find the latch and open the window, she could break the spell...

There.

The latch clicked, she pushed the window out, and...

"Saints in heaven..." Raquel whispered, now gaping at the scene beyond. Her bedchamber had given her a view of two structures and a street, but Jake's room overlooked the main entry, wall, and gate, which was cracked open like the curtain over a stage, revealing the chaos of battle beyond.

Raquel squinted, trying to make sense of what she was seeing, but the fight was all silhouettes and flying things much too large to be birds, obscured by mist and flashes of strange blue light. Figures moved along the wall, watchtower, and just inside the open gate, fighting against enormous winged creatures that were trying to claw their way through.

And saints, there were so many of them!

A kith man screamed as he was plucked from the gate's opening and pulled into the mist, and more Forest kith rushed to plug the hole he left behind. She spotted Marix by his braided hair, spinning blades and knocking back vicious wings. Why didn't they close the gate?

Unless Jake was out there.

If only she could see...

As if the Almighty himself had answered her silent plea,

the battlefront parted just enough, giving her a glimpse through the wall and to the battle beyond.

Where an entire *company* of Forest kith was trying to get through to safety.

Raquel tapped her finger upon the windowsill. This wasn't her fight. Those winged demons were *Jake's* enemy, and if they killed him, well, it might just solve a lot of her problems.

Except that horde would probably come for her next.

She wouldn't stand a chance against so many, and then she'd never figure out how to save Harran.

Another Forest kith was snatched from battle and dragged into the mist with his screams.

That decided it.

Raquel did not have magik, but she was generally good with a blade, and anyhow, she couldn't in good conscience stand back and watch. She might die, but that was true on any given day, and—in her opinion—it was far better for a person to die on their own terms than spend their life hiding in a corner, hoping death would pass them by.

Raquel spun away from the window, snagged Jake's coat and put it on, and tucked her blond hair inside of it. Not because she thought the glamour would be effective for her, but to hide her long golden hair. She grabbed all of the blades she could find, including a very long and fancy curved sword with a hilt decorated in golden vines that looked exactly like the ones inked upon Jake's biceps. Raquel smiled to herself as she secured it to her waist, then crawled through the window and dropped two stories to the ground.

The battle was much louder outside, and Raquel wondered if *sight* wasn't the only sensory detail that Jake had obscured from her.

However, no one paid her any attention. Everyone was

too busy looking toward the gate, where at least four of those ghastly winged creatures were trying to force their way through, and the horror of them up close made Raquel's blood suddenly run cold.

They had human heads, though their features were exaggerated and overgrown to the point of crudeness, and they had human-shaped torsos too, though their skin was leathery and covered in fine black hairs. But that was where the comparisons ended. Instead of arms, their shoulders morphed into thick black feathers and massive claw-tipped wings, which were currently clawing and raking at the Forest kith fighting them off.

Raquel took quick inventory of the scene and started running for the watchtower, but a new gap in the gate diverted her feet, and she soon found herself running toward Marix.

He whirled on one of the winged demons, cutting his blade across its wings, and it shrieked as it soared back into the mist. He looked over, caught sight of her, and froze. "What are *you*—"

In his shock, he hadn't noticed the winged demon descending upon him, but Raquel had, and she threw one of her many blades. Silver streaked sure and true, and it sank into the creature's chest. Its cry was cut short as it died and dropped from the air, landing at Marix's feet.

He blinked at her.

"Where's Jake?" Raquel yelled.

A smaller winged demon came down at Marix, but he noticed this one and punched it out of the way with hardly a glance. "Out there! Wait, where are you going?"

Raquel pushed through the fighters, ignoring Marix, who yelled after her, and then she was outside.

It took her a second to make sense of the chaos in the mist. Light flashed, and Raquel found herself momentarily stunned by the sheer number of winged creatures swarming above. There had to be at least a hundred! And below, working desperately to fend them off, were nearly three dozen kith. It took Raquel a split second more to spot the *real* issue.

The Forest kith's attentions were divided between the horde above and the small kith seated upon agitated horses below.

Children.

Kith children.

Raquel had never seen a kith child. She'd known they existed, of course, but what were they doing here?

Raquel counted three children in total, all attempting to calm horses that were trying so desperately to flee, which was also where she spotted Jake, spinning in a maelstrom of steel and light. He fought alongside an impressive female kith to protect the small and terrified riders from this unending onslaught of claws and wings.

Raquel stood momentarily mesmerized. Almighty in heaven! Watching him fight, she knew he had held *everything* back with her. No amount of training could have prepared her for the force that was Jake. He existed in his very own fighting class. His grace, his precision and efficiency. His *speed*. It wasn't humanly possible to move that fast, but then again, he wasn't human.

Still, Raquel could help, in her way.

She pushed on, blades in hand. Ducking and slashing as she dodged right into the melee, spinning and kicking, fighting her way toward Jake and those children and the frightened horses. Jake yelled, his swords arced down, and his gaze locked on Raquel.

He froze.

If Raquel had thought him furious before, he was positively *livid* now. Especially when he realized what she was wearing.

"WHAT IN HELL DO YOU THINK YOU ARE DOING?" he shouted at her.

"You forgot your sword, Highness." She tossed the beautiful relic at him.

He plucked it from the air, though his eyes never left hers. He appeared too stunned to respond. The fearsome kith woman he'd been fighting alongside glanced over at them as she withdrew her long sword from a demon's belly. The demon's wings flapped erratically, and it collapsed to the ground in a heap of feathers and black blood.

"I'll get the children inside! Cover me!" Raquel shouted and started for the nearest horse.

Jake's hand whipped out and wrapped around her arm like a vice, then he jerked her right back so that they were face-to-face. There was nothing friendly in his eyes. "Go back *now*."

"I will not sit in my room like a coward!"

"Better a coward than a fool! This is madness!"

"Madness is dressing up as a bear, abducting a young maiden, locking her up, and not expecting her to be upset about it."

More kith were looking over now.

"Of all the—" Jake was starting to say when another winged demon shrieked and fell from the sky. Jake pulled her one step to the right, and the creature landed right where they'd been standing. "*Get out of here*!"

"You need help!"

"Not yours!" he snarled, then yelled over her shoulder, "*Rian*! Escort my *beloved* back to her chambers!"

But before Rian could break away, one of those winged demons swooped low, and Jake yanked Raquel to the ground with him. Once clear, Jake started to rise, but Raquel spotted another shadow bearing down upon them, so she planted her feet on Jake's torso and kicked him backward instead. Jake cried out in surprise as he stumbled back, and Raquel rolled to the side. The creature struck ground, which gave Jake enough time to gather himself, swing his beautiful sword—was it glowing?—and dislodge the creature's head from its body. The head dropped, spraying black blood all over Raquel.

Raquel shoved herself to her feet and wiped the blood off her face with Jake's cape. "You did that on purpose!"

"Absolutely."

Another creature came at him, and he swung but only managed to knock the creature off course. The creature regained balance, then adjusted its trajectory in an attempt to fly at him again.

Suddenly, Jake's sword flared as white as moonlight and vanished. One second it was there, glowing in his hand. The next—gone. And then it blinked into existence up above, soaring through the air like some errant bolt of lightning. The creature didn't have time to change course, and it soared right into Jake's glowing sword, impaling itself. The creature shrieked and dropped like a stone, and the sword vanished and reappeared in Jake's fist, its light gone.

And then a child screamed.

Raquel glanced over to see the three horses holding children bolt into the trees, carrying their small riders off with them, while two—no, three winged demons altered course and flew after them.

Raquel took quick inventory of her immediate surroundings and spotted a horse, braying and bucking near its master. Without a second thought, Raquel sprinted straight for it, pushed past its master, climbed into the saddle, and kicked it into a gallop.

7

Though Raquel had executed her share of terrible ideas throughout the course of her life, this might, in fact, have been her worst. But she was desperate, and desperation led a person to do any manner of things they might otherwise know to be...well, stupid.

Like galloping into the mist full of winged demons in a land she did not know.

But saints as her witness, she could not, in good conscience, abandon those children.

She held fast to her horse as she galloped away from the battle, following the children's cries, though without the light from the outpost and bursts of magik, the forest quickly became dark and impossible to see. Raquel slowed to a trot, eyes narrowed as she strained to make sense of the shadows.

Where the devil had those demons gone? She knew she'd seen at least three take off after the children. Twice, she thought she caught a glimpse of movement, but there was nothing but mist.

And then—finally—she spotted the children. They'd

reached the dead end of a very tall, very wide embankment, their horses pacing and snorting, trying to find a way to escape. But Raquel was not watching the children. Her attention fixed on the three winged demons nearby, hovering just inches above the ground, snarling and gnashing their teeth, slowly closing in.

One lunged.

A child screamed.

Raquel threw her blade.

Right before the demonic creature snagged the child, the blade hit, but not in the place she'd intended. It sank in its lower back. Not a fatal strike, but a hindrance.

The creature wailed a horrible predatory sound, rent with bloodlust and nightmare. Its back arched as its body flexed and wings twitched, and all three demons turned toward her.

"That's right," she taunted, dismounting. "Come on…"

The one she'd struck snarled and rushed her, but Raquel was ready for it. She spun out of the way, whirled, and used her momentum to plunge a blade into its wing as it rushed past.

This time, it screamed.

"Try flying away now, you oversized rat," she murmured, and the other two came at her. She dropped, one zipped right over her, then she rolled and stabbed up, right into the reaching claws of the second. That one jerked back but didn't fly away, instead whipping its massive black wings down upon her. Raquel cried out and covered her face as feathers beat and assaulted, and then she kicked firmly back, knocking it into a tree.

To Raquel's amazement and horror, the tree's lower branches curled around the winged demon now thrashing and shrieking like a fly caught in a web. More and more branches wrapped around the demon, cocooning it completely as it drew the demon *in*to its trunk. The demon's shrieks cut short, the branches relaxed, and there was no longer any sign of the demon, but there was a very obvious bulge within the tree's trunk.

Raquel was so stunned by this carnivorous tree that she did not notice the other two winged demons were coming for her again. She managed to spin away from one, only to find herself face-to-face with the second.

And her world stopped.

Those *eyes*. They were black and soulless and terrifying, set in features so gruesomely overgrown, and yet...

The creature stared at her as she stared at it.

It blinked and tipped its head.

And then *pain*.

Fire seared in her gut as the third winged demon—the largest demon of all—withdrew its massive claws from her belly. Its bared black teeth filled her vision as she gasped and dropped to her knees while the enormous winged demon whipped around to strike her again.

But the other demon—the smaller one that had stirred something within Raquel—beat its wings at the larger, knocking it back. The large one snarled, and the two gnashed their teeth, circling each other like predators fighting over a kill.

Raquel tried to stand, tried to use their momentary distraction to slip away, but that fire flared through her limbs, her legs gave, and she collapsed just as the larger demon threw back the smaller with incredible force. The smaller crashed to the ground and did not get up again.

And the large demon approached.

Again, Raquel tried to rise, but her arms would not respond. The fire had faded to bitter cold, her body felt oddly numb, and her consciousness was quickly fading.

The last demon towered over her, all snarls and nightmares and horror.

And Raquel thought that maybe she wasn't so ready to die after all.

Suddenly, a bolt of light pierced the winged demon's chest. The demon screamed and dropped as that sword of light reappeared in its master's uniquely capable hand. Jake whirled once more and sliced the large winged demon clean through. The air reeked of burnt hair as its two halves dropped to the ground like heavy stones, and Raquel's final view was of Jake. He heaved as he stared down at her, his white tunic drenched in black blood. But then her vision tunneled, and her world faded completely.

8

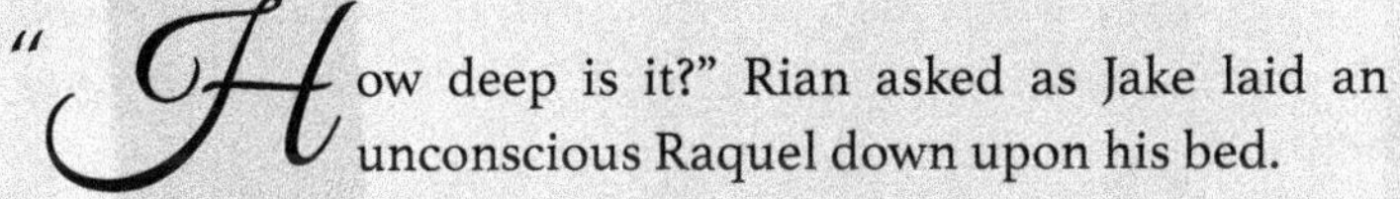

"How deep is it?" Rian asked as Jake laid an unconscious Raquel down upon his bed.

"I don't know. Help me with her clothes."

Rian was there the next instant, and together, they peeled Jake's glamoured cape from Raquel's arms.

That damned corset.

Jake forced his gaze upon her torso, where deep red blood stained the fabric that matched her brilliant summer sky eyes.

"Sit her up," Jake said, and Rian did as commanded while Jake withdrew a dagger and cut the corset's ties. He tossed the corset aside, Rian laid her back down, and—very carefully—Jake cut her slip from neckline to waist and peeled the fabric back from the wound.

Rian sucked in a breath through his teeth.

Raquel's cut wasn't deep, though it was long and bled freely—the red so bright, like everything else about her. But it wasn't the depth that concerned him. It was the oily black substance mixed with her blood. The poison of the

Depraved. One drop was enough to turn a mortal, and this was much more than that.

"Find Sienne," Jake said.

Rian didn't hesitate. He stood and left immediately, while Jake stayed with Raquel. He plucked a clean tunic from his drawer, knelt beside the bed, and held it against her wound to staunch the flow.

"What were you thinking, you insolent, foolish, *beautiful* girl."

He had not meant to speak that one word aloud, but he was so struck by the sheer *vibrance* of her. The warm hue of her skin, the natural blush in her cheeks.

The *life*.

Life isn't a game, Jake, she had said. *It is a* gift, *coveted by those who would give anything to still have breath in their lungs —breath you and your kith take for granted.* I don't have time *to take it for granted. Every second counts for me.*

"Then why are you so reckless with yours?" he said, studying her. He could truly observe her now, this mortal bride so unlike his kith even before their kingdom had been cursed. That color—that life—was what had ensorcelled him before when she'd snuck into his bedchamber.

No, before even that. When she'd stood before her people and offered herself up to him. Even for a mortal, she stood out.

Especially for a mortal.

Yes, the women of the Forest were known for their perfect beauty, yet as Jake gazed upon the mortal girl, he couldn't help but marvel at the beauty in *im*perfection. In color that blotched and shifted, in the splattering of freckles that dusted her nose and spoke of time spent in the sun. The differences marked her and set her apart and made her so deeply intriguing.

His gaze followed lines that weren't soft with privilege

but were cut with training and discipline. His attention moved to hands that weren't smoothed but were callused and strong from hard work. Raquel's nose turned up at the end, as though set in a natural state of defiance, and her upper lip jutted out more than the bottom, giving a pucker to her mouth that Jake felt the sudden urge to taste.

Which was precisely the moment Rian returned with Sienne, who was still covered from head to toe in Depraved blood.

Sienne's eyes narrowed on Raquel, and then she turned the heat of her wrath upon Jake. "You idiot. You should have known better."

"There are countless things I probably should have done, but before we begin listing off all of my deficiencies, perhaps you might consider helping the girl before she dies in the next two minutes...?"

Sienne pursed her lips but joined him at the bed. "She's a pretty little mortal, isn't she?" Sienne eyed him.

"She'll be a dead little mortal if you don't hurry."

"That's hardly my fault. Well, let me see it."

Jake pulled back the tunic he'd been holding against Raquel's wound, and Sienne fell still. She looked long at Jake, who looked steadily back, and a strange and heavy pressure settled upon his chest. "Can you help her or not?" Jake asked tightly.

"It seems I *must*," Sienne snapped. "Unless you've got another eligible mortal bride hiding somewhere in your bedchamber. It wouldn't be the first time."

Jake glowered at her, but she shooed at him. "Well, get back. I can't possibly purge the poison from her body with all this anxious energy simmering around you."

"I'm not anxious."

"Mm."

Jake regarded her flatly but stepped back to give Sienne

room while Rian—now joined by Banon and Marix—watched from the doorway. Sienne knelt beside the bed, then flipped her dark hair over her shoulders.

Jake flexed his fingers.

Sienne smoothed the blankets upon the bed.

Jake tapped his foot.

Sienne glanced back at him. "Not anxious, are we?"

"*One* minute."

Sienne rolled her eyes, took Raquel's hand in hers, and closed her eyes.

A breath.

Sienne's forehead wrinkled.

"How bad is it?" Jake asked.

"Very."

That pressure pushed harder upon his chest, making it oddly difficult to breathe. He told himself that it was because of their mission. That she was their only chance. If he failed now, he would never be admitted to the palace again, and he would spend the rest of his life running from Edom's vengeance.

Though considering the state of their kingdom, *the rest of his life* might not be very long.

Sienne murmured, and Jake felt that familiar pull upon the ether—the force that linked all Forest kith. A force they drew upon in various forms, depending upon the Fates' discretion, and the Fates had gifted Sienne with healing. In fact, she was the most talented healer Jake had ever known, and that was saying a lot. One acquired many acquaintances the longer one lived, and Jake had lived to see almost one hundred years of sunsets.

Never sunrises. He was usually still sleeping off drink from the night before.

And you... you have so much time and all the resources in the world, yet you whittle it away on drink and games *that cause the rest of us pain and suffering.*

He looked back at Raquel unconscious and bleeding in his bed. Sienne's expression wrenched with pain, the fire in the hearth flickered and dimmed, and Sienne gasped.

Something was wrong.

Jake was already walking forward as Sienne's eyes snapped open and found his.

"How can I help?" Jake asked.

"I need to borrow some of your strength," Sienne said. Her voice rattled, and she held out a trembling hand.

"Do you plan on giving it back?" Jake said with a smile, but there was no mirth in it. He was attempting to make light of a situation that was not light at all. Sienne knew it too, and she looked as though she were about to rebuke him for it, but then he held out his hand in offering.

Sienne closed her lips and took his hand.

And she pulled.

Jake dropped to his knees with a gasp. "Maybe ease into it…next time…" he managed, feeling his own life force draining from his body. Fates, how many years was she taking? Five? Ten?

Does it matter? You waste it all away anyway… He heard a small voice in his mind that sounded irritatingly like Raquel's.

Jake's head began to pound, his chest constricted, and just when he was about to yank his hand from Sienne's, she let go.

Jake sagged forward and caught himself on the edge of the bed. Sienne was similarly slumped over, skin pale and eyes closed, but Jake's attention slid to Raquel, her wound.

The oily black poison was gone, and the bleeding had stopped.

Jake breathed in fully for perhaps the first time since he'd first laid eyes on her holding Lightbringer outside the gates. He watched Raquel's soft and rounded bosom rise and fall, slow but steady. And then he wondered if staring was still considered bad manners when the subject wasn't entirely conscious.

Raquel would say yes.

The thought made him smile.

"How many years did you take?" Jake asked.

Sienne lifted her head and wiped her brow. "Near fifty."

Jake turned his head and looked at his cousin.

Sienne returned his gaze.

Jake's eyes narrowed.

"I gave her fifty of mine, too," Sienne said to his surprise, and then she returned her attention to Raquel. "Do not fail us, Jake. We've all invested our future in you."

Jake was still reeling from the fact that Raquel had needed one *hundred* kith years to pull out of that with her life. "I know. I still intend to leave at dawn."

"That could be a problem. It might take her a few days to wake."

Jake frowned. "How many days?"

"Two days. One week. It all depends on her."

They didn't have a week. "I'll have a cart prepared."

"I don't think that's a good idea," Sienne replied. "Any disruption to her present stasis could plunge her deeper into sleep, and neither of us have the years to spare for that. I'm sorry, Jake. I've done all I can, but she is still mortal, and her body needs time to heal."

Jake dragged his teeth across his bottom lip as he looked to a sky he couldn't see. Could *never* see. "This won't go unnoticed."

"Then let us both hope she wakes tomorrow," Sienne said, then added, "You might bind her, as I first advised. Next time, I will not be able to save her."

"There will not be a next time."

Sienne raised a brow. "Are you going to follow her around like a little pup?"

Jake smiled.

Sienne was not amused. She stood and looked pointedly down at him. "Don't lose sight of the mission, Jake."

Jake also stood, forcing her to look up. He felt unusually annoyed. "Goodnight, Sienne."

Sienne's lips pursed. She glanced askance at the three men by the door and started to go.

"How is little Avi?" Jake asked.

Sienne paused. "She's all right. A little shaken, but unharmed."

Then, "Why did you bring her?"

Sienne gazed back at him. Her expression had turned somber, and Jake already dreaded her answer. "I had no choice."

Jake exhaled slowly. "So Amdell has fallen."

"Yes." Sienne's gaze fell. "This is all that's left of us."

The weight of that statement filled the room with silence, for this news was heavy indeed, further compounded by the losses they'd endured this night. Amdell had been a mighty fortress, a towering defiance against the curse, and everyone expected it to fall only second to the palace. The fact that it had succumbed...

They had even less time than Jake had suspected.

"Thank the Fates your pretty little mortal doesn't do what she's told," Sienne said, pulling him from his dark and spiraling thoughts. "Reminds me of someone else I know." She gave him an emphatic look then closed the door before he could respond, leaving him alone with Raquel and his three comrades, who were studying him.

Jake made a decision. "One of you watch over her for me."

"I'll do it," Banon offered.

Jake shoved himself to his feet, then strode past his men and into the hall.

"Where are you going?" Banon called after him.

"To take a damn bath."

RAQUEL DID NOT WAKE the next morning, *or* the next, much to Jake's chagrin. It seemed to him that she defied him even in her state of unconsciousness. As if she knew he didn't have time for this, and therefore persisted in a state of deep vegetation just to get under his skin.

For *two days*.

How in the hell was he supposed to lay claim to her heart and affections while she was unconscious? Then again, at least she wasn't trying to kill him. That was an improvement.

Meanwhile, Jake's mother still had not arrived.

He could go in search of her, but he didn't dare chance missing her in the event that she appeared in his absence, and he also did not feel comfortable leaving the girl. Instead, he'd asked Astair to try again, to scry the mist and all of Canna for his mother, but to no avail. Astair could not find the queen, and this fact unsettled Jake more than any other. Of course, Jake's mother had the unparalleled talent of making herself unfindable, but she wasn't supposed to be using that talent on Jake, and certainly not now.

So where had she gone?

Hopefully his father hadn't caught wind of their plan, but each moment that passed brought Edom closer. This normally wouldn't be an issue; their plan depended upon Edom being absent from the palace, because Jake couldn't very well go traipsing into the palace as Edom with Edom still inside of it.

But that was just it: Jake needed to go traipsing into the palace as Edom to steal Edom's blessing and birthright. It was no secret that King Issachar's health had drastically declined, especially in the last year. At nearly half a millennium, King Issachar had pushed the edge of life even for their kind, and his heart had finally grown weary. It was what had prompted Jake's mother to fashion the coat in the first place, for surely King Issachar would be ready to pass on his blessing to Canna's heir this year, and with the timing of the veil—well, it was a rare moment to seize, like a gift from the Fates.

If only Jake could steal it.

But Jake needed the coat for that, and his coat was broken.

The monster that'd wounded Raquel had torn right through the fabric to get to her flesh, thus severing the intricate enchantments his mother had carefully woven. He needed that coat to enter the palace, and he needed his mother to mend the coat, or everything they'd so carefully fought for would be lost.

So Jake spent two days pacing between the watchtower, Raquel, and the forest, constantly looking out for Edom's inevitable scouts. With Banon and Rian's help, he'd burned the carnage from the night prior, glamouring the flames as best they could to hide them, and when night descended the second time and there was still no sign of his mother, he'd returned to the girl's bedside. To see if he could do anything to speed the waking process.

Havarr had left food and water for her—both untouched. Jake snatched a cracker off of the tray and shoved it into his mouth, but like everything else in this Fates-forsaken place, it tasted like dust. As flavorless as their kingdom was colorless. The only substance with any marginal flavor was wine, and so Jake washed down his bite with a large gulp from the ampoule Havarr had also left, then returned to the bedside, where he absently regarded Raquel.

Which, honestly, he found himself doing a lot. Too much, probably. But he couldn't seem to help himself. She was like a ripe fruit in this withered kingdom of rot and decay. A bolt of color in a grayscale world. A blazing fire in the bitter cold, and try as he might, he could not look away from her.

Raquel sighed and turned her face toward him, though her eyes remained closed.

She's a pretty little mortal, isn't she? Sienne had said.

No, Jake thought as his eyes slid over her face. *She is exquisite.*

Do not lose sight of the mission, Sienne had reminded him.

Jake sighed, slumped back, and raked a hand through his hair. As if he'd needed reminding. This mission was the only thing that had occupied his thoughts these last seven years, since they'd lost the last bride to the forest. Still, it was a pity that Raquel had to die.

9

Raquel's eyes opened with a start. She'd been dreaming again, as she was often wont to do. Normally, this wouldn't have been an issue, except all of her dreams had been about Jake.

Jake as a boy, doted upon by an adoring (and very beautiful) mother. To a little Jake finding comfort in his mother's arms when his twin brother had been particularly cruel and Jake's father would not hear his accusations. To a slightly older Jake being mocked and abused by a large and hairy adolescent boy who looked exactly like a precursor to the glamoured Bear Prince. To Jake spending more and more time alone in a lush and vivid forest where he could exist as he was, without courtly expectation and a barbaric twin to make his life a living hell.

Jake had memorized every plant by name and their properties. Which ones he could eat, which ones poisoned, and which could heal, and Raquel's dreams showed her many accounts of him tending to animals that his brother had tortured for sport.

And then, in her dreams, the forest began to shift and

change. A thick mist settled and anchored deep, obscuring Jake's magnificent kingdom. The light faded, and all the glorious foliage began to wither and die.

She saw Jake, his dark hair falling forward as he knelt over a stag with the largest spread of antlers she'd ever seen. The focus of her dream shifted, reeling her forward like a lure until she was standing directly behind him and gazing down upon the stag.

At the black rot covering its body and eating away at its flesh.

The stag's legs twitched as it whined in agony, and Jake's sword of light winked into existence—a single bolt of light in this strangely faded world. She watched Jake raise his sword, grinding his teeth as he yelled, and plunge his light through the stag's heart.

The stag slumped, dead.

Jake's sword winked out, his head bowed, his eyes closed, and a single tear slid down his face. In that moment, in that display of emotion he'd never given glimpse of before, Raquel's heart ached, and she was overwhelmed with the desire to wrap her arms around him. To draw him to her breast and hold him close as his mother had done.

Which was precisely what she did, in her dream.

Her arms slid around his shoulders, and she drew him in, his face to her chest. Thus supported, he sagged into her and wrapped his arms around her waist, holding so tight, and suddenly, Raquel did not want to let him go for as long as she lived.

"I can't stop it," Jake whispered against her skin, his voice shattered by grief.

In her dream, she grabbed his face between her hands and tilted it up. Stars in heaven, he was so beautiful, even more so in his grief with vulnerability spilling down his cheeks. It softened those sharp angles, melted the steel. It made this immortal kith *human*.

And his humanity was the most beautiful thing she had ever seen.

"If you truly cannot stop it, then let it go," she whispered, and bent down to kiss his full mouth. In her dream, he tasted familiar. Like comfort and warmth and safety.

Like *home*.

Jake kissed her back like a man clinging desperately to his life. As if she were the only thing keeping him from rotting away like the world all around them.

That was the moment she woke. Flushed and sweating and…utterly confused as she gazed up at a ceiling that…wasn't hers.

Even in darkness, or perhaps *because* of the darkness, she recognized the symmetry of those wooden beams, and they did not belong in her chambers.

They belonged in Jake's.

What in the devil was she doing in Jake's bedchamber…*in Jake's bed*?

She bolted upright, expecting Jake to also be in his bed with her, but she was alone. Embers glowed faintly in the hearth, softening night's shadows, but the world remained quiet. Tranquil, even.

Almighty in heaven, what in all the world…

Raquel's memories caught up to her fast: her interrupted conversation with Jake, her escape from the glamoured window (it wasn't glamoured now, she noted), her flight into the forest after the children, the strange, paralyzing moment with that creature, and Jake's sudden appearance saving her from the largest of them.

For all that Raquel had accused Jake of underestimating *her*, she had woefully underestimated *him*, and—saints above—Jake had been magnificent. Wielding that glowing sword as though he were a god wielding a bolt of lightning. It was difficult not to admire such skill, and again, Raquel was chastened by the depth of her delusion, believing she could actually overcome this forest prince.

If Lee had known, he never would have let her offer herself to the elders.

But then a thousand other questions filled her mind: What *were* those winged demons? Where had they come from, and why had they attacked? Clearly, Jake had anticipated them. Jake had told Marix he'd spared extra warriors for this reason. And then there was the issue of the kith children.

Raquel was still bewildered by them. She'd never seen a kith *child* before, and there'd been three. Which begged another question: why bring the children at all? And were they all right? *She* had made it out alive. Someone must have carried her, because her last memory was of the forest floor.

A dull ache made her glance down, and she was shocked to find that someone had washed her and changed her clothes. Her corset and heavy skirts had been replaced by a simple white nightdress made of the softest cotton. She flushed, wondering who had seen her so indecent. Was it Jake?

And then she wondered what he had thought.

Raquel could have slapped herself. In fact, she did slap her forehead just then. He might not be responsible for murdering six of Harran's young maidens, but he was still her *captor*. He'd locked her in his bedroom—he'd welded the door shut!—while demons had attacked the gates, but Dream Raquel was still fighting Awake Raquel for control over her heart. However, both became quickly distracted by the growing ache in her abdomen.

Raquel lifted her nightdress just enough to see the thin silvery scar along her belly where the monster had raked her with its claw. The scar went from naval to rib, and the wound itself should have taken *weeks* to heal. A spell of dizziness took her, undoubtedly related to that wound, and she dropped her gown and sagged back against the headboard, eyes closed. But the moment she closed her eyes, Dream Jake was there again. His tears, his vulnerability, and his warmth.

His deliciously soft mouth.

Raquel touched her fingers to her lips. She could still taste him there, a lingering sweetness on her tongue and a warmth in her heart. Prophetic dreams were nothing new for Raquel. She'd experienced them all her life, but she'd never dreamt one so...*romantic*, and this punched holes through her heart, filling them with desires for *him*. Of what could be.

Which was nonsensical!

That arrogant, selfish, heartless piece of...

She jerked her fingers away and reminded herself that the *real* Jake had stolen her away from her family, locked her in her room (or tried to), had *at the very least* been complicit in the abduction of six women, and planned to do saints-knew-what with her.

And yet.

Her dreams had never led her astray before. A few times, she'd wished they had. Like the night she'd dreamed her mother had broken her neck after being thrown from their mustang one week before it'd actually happened.

Whatever these dreams of Jake meant, the fact remained that she was the seventh sacrificial bride, Jake had disguised himself as his brother this time, and she still had no idea what he intended to do with her. He'd never answered when she'd asked, and she certainly wasn't going to get any answers while sleeping in his bed.

Well. Not the answers she needed. Where was that tricky forest prince, anyway?

Again, she remembered their kiss, the look in Dream Jake's honey-gold eyes and the taste of his lips. Saints above, Raquel could not shake that image of him—and she needed to!—so she threw back the covers and slid her feet to the floor, but she'd grossly overestimated her present state of health. Her head spun, her knees gave out, and she would have fallen if it hadn't been for the pair of strong arms that caught her.

"Careful, my bride." Jake's voice rumbled through her chest. "You're not strong enough yet."

Oh, dear. Now was definitely *not* the time.

"*Where did* you *come from*?" Raquel didn't mean to shriek at him, but he'd startled her, and the dream was still too fresh, and he was too close. Too... *everywhere*, just like he'd been in her dream, and—Almighty as her witness—she could still taste him on her tongue. "And I told you my name is Raquel!"

"Well, *Raquel*, this *is* my bedchamber," Jake said slowly, a smile to his voice. His strong arms were still locked around her, and he smelled deliciously of soap and pine and warmth. He'd also donned a fresh linen tunic, Raquel noted. "I would have placed you in *yours*; however, you seem to have developed the habit of not staying in it."

"So you took it upon yourself to put me in bed *with you*?" She glared up at him, which was a horrible mistake. His uncommonly handsome face was close enough to kiss, and that was exactly where her thoughts went.

"Calm down." His voice was thick with amusement. "Sienne will murder me if I let you pass out again. And anyway, I did not share your bed. Whatever you may think me, I've manners enough to ask a woman first, though they're usually the one's asking me..."

Raquel narrowed her eyes at him. "Scoundrel."

Those blasted dimples reappeared, which loosed a swarm of butterflies inside of her stomach, and then his features sharpened with concern. "Hm. Let's get you near the fire."

"Why?"

"You look a bit feverish."

"I'm not feverish."

He gave her a patronizing look that was becoming irritatingly familiar. "Your face is bright red and you're trembling."

She realized that she was, in fact, trembling, though she did not think it had anything to do with sickness. Still, she didn't resist as he escorted her toward the sleepy hearth. She couldn't. She didn't have the strength, but also Jake had one arm wrapped firmly around her waist. The weight of it proved a strange comfort, and his delicious heat seeped through her thin nightdress, which was all the motivation Dream Raquel needed to strangle Awake Raquel into subservience.

"How long have I been asleep?" Raquel asked.

"Two days."

"Two...*days*?" Raquel gaped up at him.

Jake snapped his fingers, and flames erupted in the hearth, bringing immediate warmth and light to the room. "You're fortunate it wasn't longer. My cousin purged the poison from your veins, and while Sienne is extremely gifted in the arts of healing, you managed to challenge even *her* constitution with the amount of poison you infected yourself with."

"You speak as if I did it on purpose..."

He eyed her sideways, a glint in his eyes. "Are you suggesting you *accidentally* stole my coat, escaped through my window—I'm still impressed by that, I might add—and charged into battle in the middle of the night?"

Raquel pursed her lips. "I did warn you."

"You did." He smirked. "Here. Have a seat...Raquel."

He'd stopped before one of the high-backed chairs situated in front of the hearth. Raquel mustered whatever dignity she had left and sat down, and once Jake appeared confident that she could sit without falling over, he sat in the chair opposite. He snatched an ampoule off the small table between them, then bent forward and filled one goblet, then the other. A lock of dark hair fell over his brow, though his gaze remained focused on the task at hand. He had large hands, she noticed. A wide palm and thick fingers that might be considered too large for his frame—the only trait that marked him as the real Prince Edom's relation—but his motions were not clunky or awkward. Every movement was precise and efficient. *Graceful.* The light of the fire warmed his skin, softening those sharp kith features, and both Dream Raquel and Awake Raquel found themselves wholly arrested by his beauty.

His gaze lifted to hers, and he raised a brow.

Raquel realized she'd been staring. Unabashedly.

She folded her arms and promptly looked to the flames, but not before catching a glimpse of his triumphant grin.

"I'm not sure what you're smirking about," Raquel said tartly.

"Mm," was his only reply, which also sounded triumphant, and then he held one of the goblets in front of her face.

"No, thank you."

"It's just water, my bride. Drink. You need it."

She meant to scold him for not using her name, but at mention of water, her mouth felt immediately parched, so she took the goblet instead. Jake leaned back in his chair, his long legs stretched and ankles crossed. The fire reflected in his eyes, making them molten, and Raquel found herself staring again, searching for the man from her dreams. The Jake with real tears and a bleeding heart. The one who made her heart ache—it ached even now. Confound it all! This would not do! She looked back to the fire and raised the goblet to her lips.

"Why did you go after the children?" Jake asked.

The goblet froze at her lips. In her dreamy, simpering stupor, she'd completely forgotten about them. "Oh, saints... the children!" She pulled the goblet away and slapped a hand over her mouth. "I completely forgot to ask...are they well? You did manage to save them, yes?"

"They are well," Jake answered firmly, as if he meant to mollify her inevitable spiral of concern.

Raquel sighed with relief. "Oh, thank the saints..."

"You are very lucky to be as well," he said with such candor that Raquel glanced back at him. His eyes bored into hers, though she could not read the expression there. "Which is why I can't figure why you risked your life to go after the offspring of your sworn enemies."

"They're *children*."

"Yes, but they're *our* children."

Raquel set the goblet on the chair's armrest. "And? I have no grievance with them simply because they are yours."

"But they *become* us."

"Is their future already decided? Have they no choice? Perhaps an act of kindness from a mortal is all they need in order to *become* something different." Raquel shifted beneath the new intensity in his gaze. She didn't quite know what to do with *serious* Jake. "Anyway, whatever their futures, they are still innocent, and I wanted to help them if I could."

Still, he studied her. "Have your...objectives changed, then?"

"I'm not sure what you mean."

He bent his legs and sat forward as he looked at her. "You are not behaving like a woman set on exacting vengeance upon the people responsible for 'murdering' her dearest friend." He made quotes in the air with his fingers around that one word.

"I'm exacting vengeance on a person, not a people, and those children had nothing to do with Adina. I won't make them suffer for what Edom has done."

"But you want Edom to suffer."

"That depends: You say Adina lives, but what of the others?"

Jake's silence was answer enough, and Raquel gripped her goblet so tightly her knuckles blanched.

"*Why*, Jake?" she demanded.

His lips parted, but then his brow furrowed and he closed his mouth. "I cannot answer that," he said a moment later.

"Cannot or *will* not?"

A muscle ticked in his jaw, and he considered her. "Is that why you took my coat? You saw an opportunity to escape, and you thought my coat would disguise you, despite my saying it wouldn't?"

"That's not why I took your coat. I took it to hide my hair"—Jake's brows shot up—"and anyway, the matter of your coat pales in comparison to the fact that five of Harran's women are now *dead* because of you!"

"Because of Edom."

"You didn't exactly help them!"

"Neither did your elders, and I don't see you exacting your *righteous* vengeance upon them."

At this, Raquel stammered and fumed. He had a point, curse him!

"Suffice it to say," Jake continued, raising his goblet and tilting it, "we all play a role in this game that is life. Edom made his moves, as did your elders. Now it is my turn." He took a sip from his goblet.

"And what, pray, is your next move, Highness?" Raquel cut back.

Jake lowered the goblet and licked his lips. "I am reevaluating at present."

"Because I've been asleep the past two days?"

He looked at her over his goblet. "More because my coat has been rendered functionally useless."

Oh. Then, "How is that?"

Jake sighed, lowered his goblet, and looked to the flames. "There's a large gash across the front that severed all of the enchantments, thanks to your little scuffle with that *oversized rat*." He glanced sideways at her.

That gash probably mirrored her new scar. "Can it be fixed?"

"By the one who made it, yes. I think."

"I imagine that person would be happy to fix it for you."

Jake turned his head and looked at her fully. "*Happy*? I don't believe my mother is familiar with the term—"

Raquel sat forward. "Wait, your *mother* made that coat for you?" To this, Jake tipped his head a fraction, and Raquel could hardly believe it! But she had to believe it, because Jake couldn't lie. "You're saying your own mother performed treason against one son in order to help the other...?"

"It's complicated..." Jake waved two dismissive fingers.

"*Complicated*? That's abhorrent!"

"I would argue that offering one's only daughter to the Forest kith in order to protect your village another seven years is equally repugnant, but we all do what we must, it seems…"

Raquel pressed her lips together. "So where is he now—your brother?"

"Probably suffering a migraine from the sedative I slipped into his drink—but anyway, you've definitely complicated matters for me."

"And those matters are…?"

Jake smiled wickedly, then lifted his goblet to his lips again.

"I see. Yet again, I've touched upon something you either cannot or will not share," Raquel chided, and Jake didn't deny it. "Well, whatever those matters are, you clearly still need your disguise."

"That does seem to follow, doesn't it?"

"Are you going to tell me *why*?"

He pulled the goblet away. His eyes shone, and a slow smile stretched his lips—so devastating that it nearly stopped her heart. "Would you believe me if I said that I find you woefully intriguing and want you all for myself?"

Those blasted butterflies filled her chest and started filling her limbs too. "No. Not in a hundred years."

"You are so consistently suspicious, my bride."

"And you already admitted that you're not in the habit of getting attached."

"People change with the right motivation."

Raquel graced him with a look of condescension, to which his smile only widened, and then he tipped his goblet toward her. "But you truly are lucky to be alive. There was a good amount of Depraved poison in your veins."

"*Depraved…* is that what you call those winged monsters?"

Jake took a small sip from his goblet. "Though I think I like your terms better."

"And what happens if one is infected with Depraved poison?"

"If one is lucky, one dies."

"And if one is *un*lucky?"

Jake's smile turned mirthless, and that kith wildness reflected in his eyes. "You become one of them."

"Oh." Again, she remembered the Jake from her dreams. The one who had said *I cannot stop it*.

Was *this* what he'd been trying to stop? This plague upon his land? A disease that rotted stags and infected the forest with mist and turned their people into Depraved?

"When did it start?" Raquel asked. It was a strange question to ask, because it followed the statement Dream Jake had made, but if real and present Jake found it odd, she couldn't tell.

"Nearly half a century ago," he answered.

Raquel stilled.

The first bride. That was when the Forest kith had first come to Harran demanding a mortal bride in exchange for protection.

Because they needed a mortal to stop whatever plagued their land. Deep in her bones, Raquel felt that to be true.

And yet this plague persisted, and they kept taking brides. No, *Edom* kept taking brides. Raquel really needed to sort this part out so that she knew precisely how to stop *Harran's* curse. She leaned forward so that she and Jake were both bent over the small table, and she asked, "How is this different?" She gestured between them. "What will *you* do with me that your brother has not already tried with six others?"

Jake's gaze bored into hers. He was not smiling now. "I will succeed," he said so softly, and Raquel suddenly realized how close they sat, the two of them bent over the small table, the fire their only companion.

Her heart beat faster, and she swallowed, determined. "*How* will you succeed?" she whispered, trying to find her conviction despite a body that was having a very different response to this handsome forest prince.

"Like this." Jake did not break her gaze, not as he set his goblet upon the table, nor as he reached out for her, slowly giving Raquel every opportunity to back away. To knock his hand aside.

She told herself to do it. To lean back and smack his hand away. He was her captor! She should not let him near, let alone touch her. But try as she might, she could not persuade herself to push his hand aside. She couldn't *move*, actually, so she sat frozen and hardly breathing, wondering what his wide palm felt like upon her skin. Wondering if it felt like the Jake in her dreams. Wondering until she didn't have to wonder.

His skin was so warm, so surprisingly gentle, even as his calluses scratched her skin. It took everything inside of her not to lean into it, because it also felt familiar when it should not have. But her soul clung defiantly to that familiarity, finding comfort in it, just as Dream Raquel had done.

Jake's gaze dropped to her mouth.

Saints, was he going to kiss her?

More importantly, was she going to *let* him?

"You're...going to save your kingdom by kissing me?" Raquel managed in that slip of space between them.

His gaze was liquid fire. "Do you want me to kiss you, Raquel?"

Her name, spoken upon his lips, brushed over her like silk, and her heart pounded. "No," she scoffed, but not even her voice believed her.

The edge of Jake's mouth curled. "No...?" He dragged his thumb over her bottom lip. "Truly? Your eyes say otherwise."

Raquel meant to respond, but she was paralyzed, and her heart galloped in her chest. What was happening? He was Dream Jake and he was *this* Jake, both versions of him flickering back and forth and never settling. He was present and future and past all at once, and Raquel couldn't break them apart. She couldn't break her *self* apart, this strange collision of dreams and reality, this merger of sacred planes.

No, it was not until Jake tipped her chin up and began to lean forward that she looked straight into his eyes, prompted by forces she could not quite understand, and said, "I do not want your kiss without your heart, my prince."

Jake stopped.

He leaned back a fraction, and his gaze met hers. His lips parted, but then his brow furrowed with confusion.

The moment stretched, and his hand was still upon her face. Raquel sat quietly, letting the silence breathe. Wondering if maybe—just maybe—it might give Dream Jake the opportunity to rise to the surface.

But when Jake's derisive smile appeared, she knew she had hoped in vain.

"I cannot give you that which I do not possess," he said.

"Then you cannot take what you have not purchased in full."

His eyes burned with something she could not identify. "My bride drives a hard bargain." A dangerous edge touched his voice.

"Bargains must be made with those whose honor can't recommend them."

His eyes narrowed. "I saved your life."

"For my sake or yours?"

Jake looked hard at her.

And then he dropped his hand.

He stood abruptly. "It is late, and I should let you rest."

Raquel looked up at him. She felt so unbalanced by the sudden shift in this interchange, and the pain of dashed hope, that she couldn't find words to respond.

He started for the door.

"What happens next?" she asked, finally finding her voice.

He stopped with his hand on the door, but he did not turn. His shoulders were tight. "We leave at dawn."

"For where?"

A breath. "I need to fix my coat, and then I'll introduce you to my father." He left and closed the door behind him.

JAKE STOPPED IN THE HALLWAY, just outside the door, and he dragged a hand over his face.

"Is everything all right, Your Grace?" Havarr asked.

Fates, he hadn't even realized Havarr was standing there, and it looked like she'd brought a pail of fresh water.

"Yes, everything is... fine," Jake said. "Just make sure she doesn't run away again."

Havarr frowned at the door. "Is she awake?"

Jake nodded and strode past a curious Havarr and shoved through the door opposite his own. "Tell the others to prepare for departure at first light," he said, then slammed the door shut, irritated that he still felt pulled to the girl.

Irritated that he felt anything at all.

10

Jake did not sleep well. In fact, he didn't sleep at all. He wasn't one for dreams. He couldn't remember ever having one, but last night he had dreamed about *her*. The mortal girl.

Raquel.

Kissing her.

Making love to her.

Fates, his heart pounded just thinking about it, and he sagged back in his bed to relive that...*intoxicating* moment, but then the rest of his dream flashed before his eyes. The two of them had stood at a window, and he'd been behind her, his arms wrapped around her full and rounded belly while his chin rested upon her head. Strangely, this simple gesture struck him harder, struck him *deeper* than anything they'd done in that bed. She'd felt like an extension of his own person, more precious to him than any lustful craving or desire.

More precious to him than his own flesh.

He'd held on to her while they'd observed two children playing in the yard beyond, picking flowers.

A girl and a boy. The girl had Raquel's beautiful thick golden hair, while the boy had his dark locks, and in the dream, Jake had been overwhelmed. He'd been flooded with a joy that'd warmed him from the inside out, as though the sun itself had been unleashed inside of his chest.

It was preposterous. A pathetic mortal dream full of futile and fading ambitions.

In fact, it was probably *his* current ambition of earning her affections that had inspired such nonsense.

And his...unspent desires from last night.

Jake pressed a hand to his bare chest, trying to massage the sudden ache out of it. He couldn't understand why it was hurting. He hadn't injured it, and yet there was an undeniable pain beneath his left breast, where a heart should be. It seemed to him that all of those emotions he'd experienced in his dream had been ripped out of his chest when he'd awoken, leaving gaping holes behind.

Which was utterly absurd. He didn't want children. He didn't even *like* children.

An image of that little girl with Raquel's tumbling golden hair flashed in his mind, that smile like the summer sun. She'd had his eyes, he remembered. Sometimes dark, sometimes gold, depending on his mood, and right then they'd been bright as autumn leaves. Effervescent. In his mind, he saw her run to him and leap into his arms, call him Father.

Say she loved him.

Those words. *Love*. Such a ludicrous notion. A weakness of mortals.

He saw his dream self cling to the child, tuck her under his chin, and hold her close. This precious treasure, so vibrant, just like her mother, and Jake felt suddenly...envious.

He dragged a hand over his face, as if he might wipe

away these new and strange and very unwanted sensations, and then slid out of bed. Fates, what was wrong with him? He was supposed to be claiming *her* affections, not the other way around. Perhaps he'd had too much wine. His mother was always accusing him of drinking too much.

Remembering his mother sobered him at once. Edom was most certainly on the move by now, but Jake could not return to the palace before his coat was repaired.

Jake dressed quickly, trying to shake his dream. Trying to ignore the persistent ache in his chest. He looked for his coat, but then suddenly recalled he'd left it in his bedchamber, where his belov—where *the mortal* slept.

Jake threw open his door and crossed the hall. He didn't bother knocking this time. He waved his hand then pushed through the door.

Where he stopped in his tracks.

The room was empty, her corset and heavy skirts gone. Obviously she'd dressed, though he did wonder how she'd managed the corset since he'd cut the ties.

Jake looked over the bed, which Raquel had taken the time to make. She'd even draped the nightdress over it, refolded the extra blankets, and neatly stacked them at the end of the bed. In fact, it almost looked as though no one had slept here, except for the presence of his coat, which she'd also folded and set upon his chair.

Jake laughed despite himself. Only Raquel would take the time to tidy up her prison before escaping it.

However.

Jake crossed to the window, where the draperies had been opened and the latch had been unlocked, and he peered outside. Dawn brightened the mist, and Jake spotted a couple of figures walking below. Neither of them was Raquel. His gaze cut to the gate.

Which hung open a crack.

Jake cursed, then sprinted from the room, bolted down the stairs, and pushed into the cold morning air. Someone called his name, but Jake didn't turn, didn't stop.

Certainly, she wasn't that foolish. He'd thought she'd learned her lesson.

Someone called his name again as he slipped through the gate and into the mist, where he knelt and touched the soil, searching for any signs of—

"What in the hell, Jake?" Rian startled him.

"She's gone," Jake said, standing so suddenly Rian had to step back to avoid being knocked over.

"What are you talking about?" Rian asked.

Jake grabbed Rian's shoulders and held them firmly. "She escaped through my window."

Rian's expression opened with understanding, and then his attention cut to the swirling mist. "I haven't seen anyone near the gate."

"Well, it's open," Jake snarled. "Who the hell was on watch?"

Rian blinked and looked back at him. "Ah... that'd be Norro, but—"

Jake released Rian, ran back through the gate, and sprinted for the stables.

Where he skidded to halt.

Raquel was there, her hair loosely pulled back in a plait, and she was dressed in her skirts and that blasted corset she'd mended with an assortment of ribbon and string. Resourceful little thing. She carried a bucket full of water, which she poured into a trough, then set the bucket down and pushed the hair back from her flushed face.

Jake's chest ached anew.

"Is that better?" she asked Vizzi, Jake's stallion. The horse's ears flickered as he snorted and nudged into her. "I know," she cooed, patting his nose. "I know. Now, let me see if I can find something for you to eat around here..."

Jake ducked back, secretly peering at her around the last stable. Rian was running up to him, but Jake raised a hand, and Rian stopped, curious but obedient. Jake looked back to see Raquel searching the stables while her skirts dragged upon the dirt, though she didn't seem to notice or care.

That ache in Jake's chest intensified.

Raquel spotted a bucket of rotten root vegetables, grabbed an armful, and dumped it before Vizzi.

Vizzi stomped a foot.

"It's not my favorite either," Raquel continued, "but it's better than nothing, and you need to eat."

Vizzi snorted at the bucket.

"Well, you can take that up with your master."

Vizzi whinnied.

"Yes, I know he's a pompous ass."

Jake cleared his throat.

Raquel looked up, startled, and that gorgeous color splotched her cheeks.

"Now, is that any way to speak of your betrothed?" Jake drawled.

Raquel snatched the bucket off the ground with a huff. "If my *betrothed* expects to be praised, he might consider behaving in a way that's praiseworthy."

"Oh, you mean like valiantly running after his beloved and saving her from being ripped to shreds by Depraved?"

Raquel strode to the water tap, set the bucket upon the ground, and pumped water into the empty pail. "Don't pretend that had"—pump— "*anything* to do with valor. You only saved my life because you"—another pump— "need me to stop whatever is plaguing your land. Not out of the goodness of"—yet another pump—"a heart you don't have."

Jake grinned. He couldn't seem to help it when he was around her. "That's quite enough water, my beloved. You're going to drown poor old Vizzi."

Raquel stopped pumping and looked at Jake. Her hands still gripped the lever, her cheeks were pink with exertion, and her blue eyes shone as clear and brilliant as the sky. Tendrils of hair curled about her face, dirt stained her hem and hands, and Jake had never seen a sight more lovely.

The pain in his chest nearly doubled him over.

"And *you're* going to kill him if you keep running him like this," she snapped. "For one who prizes *living* above all else, I would expect you'd take better care of your possessions."

Jake regarded her. "You're right. Next time, I'll board up your windows."

Raquel's nostrils flared, and she went back to pumping water. Jake flitted two fingers, and the lever started pumping on its own accord.

Raquel fought with the lever, but to no avail. "Would you stop?"

"I'm trying to help you, beloved."

"I don't...want your...help. And stop calling me beloved!" Raquel finally let go, flustered and arms akimbo as the lever pumped autonomously, slowly filling the bucket. "Let me do this!"

"Why, when magik can do the work?"

"But I *want* to do the work!"

Jake scoffed. "*No one* wants to work."

Raquel stomped toward him and stood right in his personal space, making him feel a sudden onslaught of very powerful things he could not identify. "That's the problem with you. With *all* your kind. So puffed-up on your magik. As if it makes you so much better and wiser than the rest of us *simple mortals* and our *pathetic ideals*. And look what all your magik has gotten you: a rotten land full of monsters and bleeding trees. So forgive me if I trust the work of my own hands over all the magik of a people who couldn't even use it to save their own kingdom."

Jake leaned in close, their faces mere inches apart. Her freckles were darker when she was angry. Or maybe they just stood out more against her angry flush, and he felt the sudden urge to continue what he'd started last night, though he was very aware of Rian—and now Banon—watching them. "Careful, my beloved." Truthfully, he didn't know if the warning was for her or for himself.

"Or what?" Her blue eyes stormed with conviction.

Jake couldn't remember the last time he'd seen a storm. A real, actual storm with brooding clouds and booming thunder, but he thought that if a storm could ever manifest itself as a person, it would come as Raquel. It would defy nature with its fury, inspire awe with its brilliance.

Destroy everything he had so carefully constructed.

His gaze dropped to her dainty nose, particularly the smattering of freckles along the narrow bridge. They reminded him of the stars in the night sky and all the constellations that he had not seen in ages. And then his gaze slid further still, to her mouth and the pucker of those chapped and rosy lips that he had meant to kiss last night.

It was the mission—yes, that was what it was. He was playing a part so well and so thoroughly that his subconscious kept him resolutely in character. But then his dream flashed again. Her rounded belly, the feel of her in his arms.

The feel of her in his *heart*.

Jake's chest ached sudden and sharply, his breath came in frantic bursts, and then for reasons Jake could not quite comprehend—not yet—he turned on his heel and stormed away from her. Right past a startled Rian and Banon.

“Where are you going?” Rian called after him, clearly confused.

“To find Sienne.”

11

Raquel watched Jake go. She watched him storm away from her, watched his kith stare after him. Watched him turn out of sight.

And then Rian and Banon turned toward her.

Raquel felt a sudden flare of embarrassment, as if she'd been caught doing something she ought naught, though she'd done nothing untoward.

Not on the outside, at least.

But they were still looking at her, so she pressed down her skirts, and—not knowing what else to do—said, "I can help with the horses."

Rian looked to Banon, whose gaze flickered in the direction Jake had gone.

"I am quite familiar with them," she continued. "I grew up around them, and I've a lot of experience fitting saddles." She didn't really understand why she felt so adamant about this, but there were all sorts of strange emotions churning inside of her, and hard work was always the best remedy for controlling unwieldy feelings.

And she needed to get these under control before they shredded her resolve to pieces.

At last, Banon nodded once, sharply, and said, "I'll handle Vizzi. Jake's very particular about his saddle."

"Really? Does he realize the bit's too tight and damaging poor Vizzi's molars?"

Banon's brows shot up, he and Rian exchanged a long look, then Banon waved a hand at Vizzi. "He's all yours. But know that if Jake complains, I'm not taking the blame."

"If he doesn't, I hope you don't take the credit, either," Raquel said.

Banon looked at her as if he couldn't decide whether to be impressed or offended. Rian laughed, then cuffed Banon on the shoulder and said, "Come on. We've only got ten minutes."

Banon and Rian moved to other stalls, and Raquel turned back to Vizzi, who regarded her mildly.

"Now. Where were we..." she murmured to herself. Then, to Vizzi, she said, "You eat. I'm going to make some adjustments to your saddle."

She slipped around Vizzi, patting his side as she did, to where the saddle lay upon a narrow bench. It was a fine saddle; she hadn't had a moment to appreciate the craftsmanship before while riding in the arms of her brutish captor.

The thought of sharing a saddle with Jake, *as himself* and not as the hairy Bear Prince, sent a shiver down her legs.

Saints above, this would not do!

Raquel ground her teeth and turned her focus back to the saddle, to the neat line of stitches and oiled leather. "If only your master took half as good care with you as he does his saddle..." She'd said it quietly, but not quietly enough. Rian cleared his throat from a few stalls over. Raquel bent her head toward Vizzi's ear and whispered, "Well, it's true."

She found the harness and bit beside the saddle, noting a number of broken stitches in the leather and a stress crack in the mouthpiece. She sighed. "Well, I don't have time to fix all of this properly, but I can loosen the tension a bit to give you some relief. Does that sound all right?"

"You know he can't understand you, right?" Rian said over the stalls.

"He understands more than you think," Raquel replied, but as she turned, she spotted a little kith girl hovering behind a nearby post, watching her.

It was one of the three from that night. One of the children that Raquel had run after.

Thus caught, the little girl ducked out of sight. Raquel waited, hoping, perhaps, the little girl might make herself known, and then Raquel spotted movement above, in the loft amidst the hay bales.

She didn't turn to look this time but noted a small shadow up above, observing her from behind the hay. Curious.

Raquel smiled to herself but got to work, feeling those eyes all the while. She slipped the saddle and harness on the horse, and she had just finished adjusting the bit when the child ducked away. The next second, she felt someone's presence directly behind her.

She didn't appreciate the effect it had on her body.

"You've collected an audience, I see," Jake mused.

"Yes," she said, finishing one last adjustment. "Apparently, hard work is a rarity around here, and everyone gathers to watch."

He chuckled.

Raquel looked back to see Jake leaning against the stable doors, his arms folded over his chest, his glamoured coat slung over one arm. Whatever had left him so uncharacteristically addled earlier was gone. His eyes were back to being warm as honey, and those full lips curved with something that made her heart stutter.

"*You* saddled my horse?" he asked.

She didn't like the condescension in his voice. "And it's a good thing too. Has no one ever taught you how to fit a harness?"

"His harness is fine."

"For an amateur."

He smirked, pushed himself from the door, and approached, then stopped so close his arm brushed hers as he bent forward to check her work. He looked over all the straps and fastenings, standing far too close for Raquel's comfort, but Raquel could not bring herself to step away.

"You loosened the harness," he said.

"Yes, well, you've over-oiled the leather. The stitching is rotting out here and here"—she pointed to each in turn—"and then you overcompensated for this by tightening the straps, which has put undue pressure on the mouthpiece... see where it's cracked?"

Jake looked from the metal to her, and Raquel's cheeks warmed.

"Anyway, I don't have time to fix it," she continued, "but I've made adjustments that should keep dear Vizzi mostly comfortable. At least until we get to....where are we going?" She let her words dangle, hoping he'd answer.

But he only stared at her, a glint in his eyes, as he said, "I see swordplay isn't the only hobby you found."

"I was raised with horses. My father kept studs, and I often helped him break in the foals."

Still his eyes were on her, and Raquel's heart beat an erratic rhythm in her ears.

"There you are!" A woman's voice slammed through the moment like a gavel.

Jake abruptly stepped away from Raquel as a woman

stepped into view. It was the same woman from the battle, the one Raquel had seen fighting beside Jake, and she was probably the most stunning woman Raquel had ever seen. Her long dark hair was plaited and draped over one shoulder, and she had the physique of a warrior but the grace of a queen, a strong nose and high cheekbones and eyes that cut like the blades she had wielded.

"Sienne," Jake said, and she stopped at attention a few paces before them.

"You said ten minutes."

"And?"

"It's been twenty."

Jake raised his gaze to the rafters. "Meet my cousin, Sienne."

Sienne.

Raquel's lips parted, and she took a step toward the woman. "*You're* the one who purged the Depraved poison from my veins."

Sienne leaned back as if overwhelmed—and maybe even spooked—by Raquel's warmth and sincerity. Meanwhile, Jake looked as though he was fighting back a smile.

"I am," Sienne admitted, though both her tone and posture were careful. As if she feared that by speaking, she was entering into some agreement she wanted no part in.

Regardless, Raquel extended her hand. "I wanted to thank you. For saving my life."

Sienne looked at Raquel's hand, then her eyes. "You saved my daughter. We're even." Her gaze flickered absently to the loft, where Raquel knew a little girl was hiding, and then Sienne turned to Jake and said, "We are ready."

12

"I must confess," Jake said to Raquel as they rode a steady pace through the mist and trees. He sat behind her in the saddle, one arm wrapped around her waist, the other holding fast to Vizzi's reins. "I am grieved to hear that my beloved bride finds her new kingdom...wanting."

He didn't sound grieved in the slightest.

"*Grieved*? Why, my dear prince, such feelings require a heart." She eyed him over her shoulder, but he flashed that devastating grin, and she promptly looked ahead again. "And anyway, what does it matter what I think?"

"*What does it matter*?" He feigned offense. "You are my bride, and nothing is more important to me than your happiness."

Raquel couldn't help it. She laughed. So loudly, in fact, Banon glanced over at them from where he sat upon his own horse.

Jake's arm tightened around her waist, sending a little (and unfortunately pleasant) thrill through her body. Especially when his chest pressed to her back and he lowered his mouth to her ear and whispered, "I have something for you."

Before she could wonder or find the voice that had suddenly abandoned her, Jake presented a red rose.

She stared at the flower, at this brilliant bolt of color made more vibrant amidst the surrounding grays. Its silken petals bloomed in full, and its sweet perfume filled her nose. She inhaled deep, in awe and in wonder, then caught herself.

Jake's coat had invoked senses as well.

"Is this a glamour?" she asked.

"No. Touch a thorn if you like. Glamour is uniquely persuasive, but I promise you it can't draw blood."

She believed him. Then, "Where in the world did you find this?"

"That, my bride, is a secret." His voice was as silken as the petals.

"Your entire life is a secret," she managed.

"Well, this little secret is yours." He held the rose closer.

She almost reached for it. "Why are you giving me this?"

He chuckled. "Always so suspicious."

She glared back at him which—yet again—was a mistake. He was too close, and his arm still encircled her waist, and she could not look at him without thinking of last night. Of the look in his eyes when he'd nearly kissed her.

"Is it too much to believe that I simply wish to court my bride?" he asked, as if taking great joy in her discomfiture.

"Then where were these *exemplary* manners before?"

"Do you mean when you were trying to murder me in my sleep? I have, on occasion, misinterpreted a woman's feelings for me, but I didn't think it a good idea to parry your blow with a flower."

Raquel grinned despite herself, and then he grabbed her

hand and set the rose inside of it, careful so that the thorns did not prick her skin.

Their gazes met.

"Tell me you do not appreciate my gift," he said. "Tell me, and I will take it back." His words caressed her, and she could not—for the life of her—deny his gift.

But then she remembered their conversation from the night before. When he'd said she drove a hard bargain. "I will not bargain for a kiss, my prince."

He smiled, all charm and innocence. "This is no bargain, my bride. As I said: it is a gift."

"You told me life is a game; therefore, I am left to conclude that you do not give freely. There is a reason."

"You're right." Mischief danced in his eyes, but then he looked ahead to the mist and the trees.

Raquel glanced down at her rose, swaying with Jake as they rode. She trailed her thumb over a little thorn and —*ouch*—yes, it was definitely real. She shoved her thumb in her mouth and sucked the fresh blood from her skin.

"An expert with blades but can't handle flowers..." Jake mused, and Raquel whacked him on the leg.

Or tried to. He caught her wrist with those lightning-quick reflexes of his and examined her injured thumb.

"It's fine," Raquel insisted. "It's just a prick. Hardly anything to..."

Her words evaporated as he pressed the pad of her thumb between his lips, right against his teeth. His eyes fixed on hers, dark as amber, and Raquel went rigid. Not because she was afraid or because she didn't like it.

But because she *did.*

Far, far too much.

The heat of his mouth was...oh, saints above, it was delicious. She could think of no other word, and when his tongue slid against the wound, her lips grew envious. Her entire body grew envious. His eyelids slid shut, but only for a moment, and when he opened them again, they looked hazy with sleep, or maybe too much wine. He dragged his mouth away from her thumb and asked, "Better…?"

Raquel swallowed, feeling flush all over as she looked at her thumb. The little prick was nowhere to be found.

He put his mouth to her ear and said, "I told you it was real."

Raquel was not so sure what they were talking about anymore, but Jake turned his attention back to their journey and said something to Banon about altering course, and Raquel sat quietly with her very confusing thoughts.

What in the blazes was going on? She'd been so resolved this morning. So resolved to be patient and learn everything she could while traveling with Jake so that when the opportunity arose, she could sneak away and seek her vengeance on the man who deserved it—Edom. Every moment between here and then was simply a means of reaching that aim. It was her own sort of game. There was no room in that game for romantic detours, no matter how *delicious* they seemed to be.

Especially with the man who had abducted her!

She had half a mind to toss his rose into the wood, but then she thought Jake's entourage might consider it a sign of disrespect toward their venerated prince, and also, it was too pretty. It seemed wasteful to sacrifice such rare beauty to a rotten wood, so she kept the rose and secured it to the ties of her corset where she'd previously kept a blade.

The hours passed on, and the mist did not relent. However, Jake kept a steady pace, guiding their company through a maze Raquel could not unravel. It all looked the same to her. Hazy fog and spindly black trees with the occasional cry of a Depraved, and she was very thankful for

Jake's expert navigation. She would not have made it through this wood otherwise.

There were nearly three dozen in their company: seven from the outpost, but the rest had come with Sienne. From scattered conversation, Raquel had learned that Jake meant to keep the bulk of his forces in Little Mignon—the outpost—but those he'd left behind would follow once he gave *the signal*, whatever that was. A few of Sienne's company had stayed back as well, including the three children. Why Sienne had brought them at all, Raquel couldn't get a clear answer, but Sienne seemed relieved that they were there.

Jake was just guiding Vizzi up the steep slope of a dried riverbed when Raquel pointed to a large mass atop the ground a few dozen paces away and asked, "What is that?"

Jake followed her finger with his eyes, and then he drew Vizzi up short.

"We stopping for the night?" Banon asked, coming to a halt behind them. "Because my arse is starting to hurt, and—"

Jake raised a hand, and Banon stopped talking.

"Wait here," Jake said to Raquel, and he dismounted.

"*Excuse me*," she snapped, swinging her leg over and jumping down from the saddle. "But I am the one who saw it, and you can't expect—"

Jake covered her mouth with his hand, and his expression warned. He glanced pointedly to the trees above, to the branches swaying strangely in a breeze that wasn't there, and he looked directly back at her, his meaning clear: Be quiet.

She glowered at him.

He gave her another very pointed look, this one asking: If I remove my hand, will you cooperate?

She answered with a look of her own that said: Yes, but I'm not climbing back in that saddle.

Jake sighed, resigned, then pulled his hand away. Satisfied that she wasn't going to argue, he gestured at Banon and walked on while the rest of their company slowly caught up.

Raquel licked her lips and followed after Jake. She'd made it halfway to the mound when she froze in her tracks.

It was a stag with a very impressive spread of antlers.

A chill swept over her skin, head to toe. The stag lay on the ground panting, each breath a struggle, and pain shone in its large round eyes.

Half of its flesh had been eaten away.

Raquel stared in horror. This was even worse than her dream. It looked as though the stag were being eaten alive, its body consumed by some pitch-like black substance that had already eaten through two of its legs to the bone and left half of its ribcage exposed to the elements.

Almighty in heaven...

Jake dropped to his knees on the ground, a somber set to his shoulders.

In a flash, Raquel saw the Jake in her dreams. The one with his head bent and vulnerability spilling down his cheeks. However, this time, Banon was there, and *this* Jake was not crying.

But there was a deep and touching sadness in his eyes.

Raquel resisted the urge to go to him as Dream Raquel had done. Her dreams were always different. Sometimes showing events as they had or would happen. Sometimes showing poetic interpretations of a moment.

This was obviously the latter.

She watched Jake as he placed his palms to the stag's exposed ribs, as he slid them tenderly along the stag's spine, murmuring things Raquel could not hear. A creak overhead drew her attention to the trees, where those branches grew bolder, searching and reaching like serpents, as if seizing an opportunity.

Jake's head was still bowed, and Banon did not notice.

"Jake," Raquel said quietly, not wanting to disrupt this moment and whatever Jake was doing but also needing to get his attention.

Those branches reached lower, curling and twisting like vines. Something snagged her hair.

She jumped away and shrieked, "Jake!"

Jake looked back at her, his eyes widened then narrowed, and he thrust his palm forward. A burst of air blasted forth, scattering dead needles and leaves until it pushed right over Raquel with so much force that her braid whipped straight back like a golden pendant.

There was a soft, keening hiss, like hot embers doused with water, and all of those reaching branches snapped back to their proper places.

Jake stared hard at her, as if checking for signs of injury. Satisfied, he looked back to the stag.

Raquel let out a shuddering breath and approached.

If Jake heard her, he didn't show it. His hands were on the stag, his eyes closed as he murmured strings of words in a language Raquel did not know but found beautiful. A grim Banon stood over them, his eyes now trained on the trees, but when Raquel neared, he acknowledged her with a stiff nod.

Jake stopped murmuring, and Raquel felt a sudden ripple of power. A push of warmth and heat and energy. The stag fell still, finally at peace, its eyes staring blankly, its head slumped.

Jake bowed his head, and he didn't move.

Banon turned away, caught Raquel's gaze, and gestured for her to follow. To leave Jake alone, to give him space. Raquel glanced at the others, then back at Jake, at the cursed stag lying dead on the ground at Jake's knees.

I cannot stop it.

Raquel slipped the rose from her corset, stepped around Jake, and lay the rose upon the stag.

When she glanced back, Jake's eyes were open and fixed upon her.

She opened her lips to say something, to bring comfort as Dream Raquel would have done, but she was not Dream Raquel, and he was not Dream Jake, and so she closed her mouth instead, letting the rose give all the comfort her words could not. She started back for the group, but as she passed Jake by, he grabbed her hand and held it tight.

She glanced down at him, and he looked up at her, his eyes darker than she had ever seen.

"Thank you," he whispered.

Raquel's heart melted a little.

She nodded once, he released her hand, and she walked on, back to the others, while trying not to dwell on all her other dreams of him.

The dreams of things yet to come.

13

Jake didn't stop Vizzi again until the sun set. It had been a quiet ride after the stag. Its death loomed like a dark cloud over them all, following them through the mist and trees. Raquel wanted to ask. She wanted so badly to know what that black substance was, how the stag had been infected, and *why*. And what Jake had done to let it pass in peace.

But she didn't.

Jake sat so rigidly behind her that she worried any conversation might make him crack. Might fracture his resolve and his composure, and though this Raquel did not mind if it shattered him to pieces, Dream Raquel would not allow it.

Actually, that wasn't quite true. This Raquel *did* mind, and that bothered her most of all.

They did not cross any other creatures, unless one counted a centipede. A forest of this size should have been a refuge for any number of wildlife, but there was nothing. Just how much of the forest life had this plague claimed?

It was in a small clearing that Jake stopped their group.

He studied the surrounding trees, his kith features all sharp lines and hard planes, his gaze narrowed. "We'll make camp here," he announced and dismounted.

Raquel, however, wasn't so sure. "What about the Depraved?" She climbed down from Vizzi, who shifted, agitated.

But Jake only gave her a dismissive, "We'll be fine," walked over to Banon, and the two of them spoke in low voices while the rest of the group caught up.

Beside her, Vizzi snorted, and his ears twitched.

Raquel reached up and rubbed the breadth of his nose. "I know. I don't much like it either."

"I thought we were staying in Drava," Sienne said once she caught up. She did not sound pleased.

"We don't have time," Jake answered, his tone clipped. He'd crouched at the edge of the clearing and was drawing in the dirt with his finger.

"We make time," Sienne replied.

"Can you extend the day?" Jake cut back. The tension in his posture edged his voice too. "Can you hold back the night and give us time to pass through Drava's gates?"

Sienne's lips thinned. A few in her company glanced sideways at her, but everyone looked resigned.

Even Sienne.

Jake stood fully and turned to face her. Gone was the mischievous, tricky prince. In his place stood an imperial and dangerous ruler. "No? Then perhaps you might make yourself of use and help me draw a perimeter so that the Depraved do not rip us to shreds as we sleep."

Sienne scowled, looked to the kith man beside her, nodded once, and dismounted. The rest of her company followed suit.

Jake, however, turned back to his task and resumed drawing symbols upon the earth.

Raquel leaned in to Vizzi and whispered, "Wait here." Vizzi snorted his disapproval, but Raquel patted his nose and slowly approached Jake.

He still crouched, his back to her as he drew symbols in the dry earth, clearing needles and leaves when necessary. He did not turn or look or verbally acknowledge her when she stopped behind him, but Raquel noted a slight hitch in his movement.

"How effective are drawings compared to stone walls?" she asked.

Jake finished a line, then scrutinized his work. "Effective enough." A pause. "Though I might advise you keep low to the ground lest one of them rip off your head."

Raquel's eyes widened.

Jake glanced at her over his shoulder, and a mischievous grin twisted his lips.

Raquel realized he was teasing and narrowed her eyes. "Scoundrel."

That grin spread, as if he proudly accepted the designation, and then he got back to work. Sienne had begun drawing symbols on the other side, the two of them working together to form a circle wide enough for all of their company and the horses. The others began unpacking and setting up camp, and Raquel felt suddenly useless.

"Is there any way I can help?" she asked.

Jake stood—still, with his back to her—took a few steps to the right, and crouched again. "Yes. Don't run away."

"I have no desire to be eaten by a tree."

Jake grunted a laugh, though the sound lacked his former lightness.

Then, "I'm sorry about the stag."

His motions snagged again, and it took him a second to cut them free. "Why? Did *you* set the curse upon him?"

So it *was* a curse! Not simply a disease. "No, but I am to stop this curse, aren't I?"

Jake stopped drawing, and he looked back at her. Raquel couldn't read the expression there. "Yes, my bride. Yes, you are."

He turned away and resumed drawing his symbols in the earth.

Raquel felt a prick of unease, and she would have asked him to expound on this new admission, but then Rian was there, holding a small cloth pouch before her.

"Eat," he said.

She peeled her gaze from Jake and glanced down at the pouch. Rian mistook her hesitation for mistrust, then withdrew a pale cracker and took an overlarge bite.

"Thee?" he said, mouth full. "Ith not going to kill you."

"*Swallow*," Raquel urged, to which Rian rolled his eyes and swallowed. Pleased, Raquel took a cracker from the pouch. "Thank you."

Rian grumbled, and he walked on to share with the others, while Raquel ambled away, still within the confines of the perimeter Jake and Sienne were drawing, and sat down upon the soft earth. She took a bite of the cracker and nearly spit it out. It tasted like sand, and actually, she *would have* spit it out, except that it had suddenly morphed into a thick paste, and she could not physically dispel it from her mouth.

"Here," Jake said with a chuckle and held his flask before her.

She meant to reply, but then her tongue stuck to the roof of her mouth, and she could not pry it free. Resigned, she took the flask from Jake's hand and washed the rest of the cracker down. Surprisingly, the wine burst with flavor. Like roses and berries and temptation.

"I can suddenly understand why you've taken to drinking," Raquel said as she pulled the flask away and dragged the back of her hand across her lips.

Jake grinned, but it wasn't easy like before, and then he snapped his fingers.

Suddenly, an enormous and luxurious sky-blue blanket appeared on the ground beneath her, and Raquel gasped in surprise. "What...how...?"

"I cannot have my bride sleeping directly upon the dirt, now can I?" Jake said.

Raquel looked around at their camp, at everyone lying directly upon the ground. "Everyone else is."

"Everyone else is not my bride." Jake stepped around her, onto the blanket, and sat down. "I may be a scoundrel, but I like to think I'm a mannerly one."

Raquel snorted.

He leaned back upon his hands, his legs stretched before him, and his sun-gold eyes fixed on her. "Tell me you disagree." There was a challenging glint in his gaze that had been gone since the stag, and Raquel was glad to see it'd returned. She didn't quite know what to do with the silent and formidable forest prince.

Because it made Dream Raquel want to comfort him.

"No, but you're still a scoundrel," she teased.

"And *you* still have my flask." He held out a hand.

She realized that she was, in fact, still holding on to his flask. She eyed him, then smirked, and took a long and deliberate sip. Jake's hand remained outstretched, though his eyes darkened, and when she handed back the flask, his lips curled in a way that made her heart jump.

Until he shook his flask and realized it was empty. "All of it? *Really*?"

"No manners, remember?" She held two fingers at her heart as he had done.

Jake's smile turned vicious, and his eyes burned with

something that nearly stopped her heart altogether. "Yes," he said lowly. "I remember." But then a crease formed between his brows, and he glanced to the trees and waved a hand over his flask before lifting it to his lips again.

"How do you do that?" Raquel asked.

Jake pulled the flask away and licked his lips. "Do what?"

"Make things appear out of thin air?"

He smirked. "Those are fiercely protected kith secrets, my bride."

"Like your curse?" She hadn't meant to bring it back to this, but it was the question that had been brimming just below the surface ever since she'd entered this strange and rotting kingdom. A question he kept maneuvering around, but it would not be ignored.

Not now.

Especially not now.

Her question settled between them, as thick and cold as the surrounding mist. Jake's entire physiognomy changed, and Raquel suddenly regretted her words—regretted calling back that dark and dangerous forest prince.

But she needed an answer; she needed to know. Unfortunately, she had been so distracted by him—by *this*, whatever it was—and confused by her dreams that she kept forgetting to persist. To get the answers she needed so that she could stop Canna's curse from plaguing her people.

"What happened to that stag, Jake?" Raquel asked quietly, though she realized the others were watching them now, listening. "Why are these trees dead but also alive? Where did your Depraved come from, and why is there no *color*?"

The camp had fallen completely silent, all of them looking to their prince to see how he would answer. To see what he would say.

Worried about what he would say.

Jake absently turned that flask in his hand, his gaze fixed ahead but unseeing. "You ask questions that I cannot answer."

"Again, I ask you: cannot or will not?"

He looked sharply at her, his gaze predatory. "Life is a game, my bride. We win some. We lose some. And we drink" —he raised his flask in toast—"to endure it all."

Raquel frowned, and he lifted the flask to his lips.

"That's it?" Raquel snapped, irritated. "That's all you have to say?"

Jake tipped back the flask and drained it.

The others still watched, though they tried not to appear like they were. A few uneasy glances were exchanged.

"It's not as simple as that, though, is it?" Raquel persisted. "I saw you with that stag. You *felt* that loss. You feel it now—you feel all of it—which is why you drink far more than you should—"

"You can't leave well enough alone, can you, my murderous, thieving virgin bride?" Jake cut her off, a smile on his lips, but his eyes were full of fire.

Raquel might have been afraid, but she was mostly irritated by his last qualifier. "Leave it alone? It's only what's plagued my people for forty-two years!"

Jake tipped his head, and that fire burned. "Plagued? You mean losing six young maidens?"

His tone suggested her *loss* wasn't loss at all, and it rankled her. She ground her teeth together. "*One* is too many, Your Grace. Just because you whittle your life away with your games and drink doesn't mean that others are content to throw away theirs."

In retrospect, she might have pushed too far with that last comment. Banon twitched forward, ready to defend his prince's honor, but Jake held up two fingers, his dark gaze fixed on hers.

"I agree," Jake said at last, his voice low and smooth and dangerous. "One *is* too many. Would you care to know how many we have lost?"

"Your people are your responsibility, not mine. I am here because—"

"Tens of thousands."

Raquel stopped. There was no humor in Jake's gaze now, nothing bating. His words were a bleeding wound—a wound carried by every person in that camp. Raquel's gaze settled on Sienne, and Sienne did not look away. Raquel had wondered why Sienne had brought her own daughter to Little Mignon, but perhaps Sienne had not had a choice.

At last, Sienne looked away.

"So forgive me if I seem *callous* and *unfeeling* concerning your *six*," Jake continued quietly, but no less firmly. "I would easily triple that number if it meant I could save my own."

Raquel held his gaze. "But we are innocent."

"So are mine."

A beat. "*I* am innocent."

His lips twisted sardonically. "Are you now, my murderous, thieving...*beloved* bride?"

Raquel scowled. "I think I am done with your little games."

He looked delighted by this profession, as if it were a challenge to be won, and he sat up straight. "I don't think you are."

"I promise you I—"

"Riddle me this, my bride," Jake cut her off again, new fire in his eyes, as if her dismissal had simply thrown kindling on open flame. "If you can solve it, then you have won, and the game is over."

Silence.

"You know what... I've had quiet enough of this—" Raquel started to push herself from the blanket.

"'*A mortal heart, the heir must claim,*'" Jake said, stopping her. "'*A babe wrought by harvest's light—*'"

"Jake..." Sienne warned.

"'*—and virgin be by immortal's sight,*'" Jake continued, his eyes never leaving her face, "'*who holds the only road to our salvation.*'"

Jake finished, and the camp was silent.

"That is your riddle, my beloved bride," Jake added. "Should you answer correctly, you will have won." He leaned forward and winked. "And you'll probably also forfeit your reason for drinking, unless one prefers to celebrate, which I do."

Raquel's frown deepened, and she would have accused Jake of making up the verse, but based on the tension that had settled over their camp, she did not think he was misleading her. Also, she knew at least part of that was true for certain. It was how Harran's elders had chosen brides: A babe wrought by harvest's light, and virgin be by immortal's sight. Everyone in Harran knew that part.

But the rest...

Jake watched her as if daring her to figure it out. Because this was their riddle. Their *curse*. He had not given her an answer—not exactly. He had given her a question instead.

"A mortal heart..." she murmured, starting from the beginning, and his eyes gleamed, enthralled that she was playing along. "Well, that's obvious." She gestured at herself. So was the part about a virgin born at harvest, but she didn't much feel like saying that aloud.

"But you're not the heir," Raquel said instead.

Jake's eyes darkened. "*Yet*."

More glances were exchanged.

Something else clicked into place, and she started thinking out loud. "That is why you need the coat. With it, you can pretend to be Edom, but you're still not the heir unless you somehow manage to convince your father to transfer kingship…"

Jake's answering smile was slow and dangerous, confirming that she was on the right track.

"*Jake*," Sienne hissed.

"And what else?" Jake prodded, his eyes only on Raquel.

"Is your father old?" Raquel asked.

Jake's eyes shone with delight. "Very."

Raquel inhaled deeply, trying very hard not to be knocked off course by the intensity in his gaze. What was the rest of his riddle? Something about claiming a mortal heart and a road to salvation…

"The heir must claim a mortal heart…" Raquel continued, then stopped. "That is your reason. You need to claim my affection to save your kingdom."

His amber eyes danced. "Bravo, my bride, so tell me: Are you in love with me yet?"

His words were easy, but his posture was not, and every single person in that camp sat utterly still.

Raquel felt a prick of unease. "I don't think you're telling me everything."

"No?" The word challenged. "Why else do you think I intervened? You've seen what my brother looks like. Who could possibly fall for *that*? He's already failed to claim the hearts of the six mortal brides before you."

Raquel stared at him, unable to shake the feeling that she was missing something extremely important, which was compounded by the uneasy expressions all around them.

Jake shoved himself to a seated position and leaned in close. His eyes were like two embers. "Edom has failed us. Look around you. My kingdom will not survive another seven years of this curse. They know this; that is why they have come." He gestured at the others. "Each time Edom fails, we fall deeper into depravity. More of us are lost."

"The Depraved," she whispered.

The pervasive silence was answer enough.

Almighty in heaven. And he had said tens of *thousands*.

"You say you must claim my heart," Raquel continued after a moment. "*And what else*?"

Jake's smile was slow and brilliant, and then he took her hand and brought it to his lips. "Tell me you do not wish to give it."

Raquel suddenly found it difficult to focus. Especially with his thumb strumming her knuckles as they were. "You did not answer my last question."

"If you'll recall, I've answered none of your questions. *You* did." He kissed the back of her hand, but he did not pull away. His lips lingered there, spreading warmth through her chest and all the way to her feet, his eyes fixed on her. "It is late, my bride," he said at last, releasing her hand. "And we've another long day of travel ahead of us. I should let you rest."

"But I'm not..."

Jake lay upon the blanket, on his side, his back to her.

For a moment, Raquel simply sat there utterly confused as she stared at his profile, at the long lines and rounded muscle. She glanced over her shoulder and caught Rian's gaze, but he turned away and lay down. The others slowly did the same, the camp settling in for the night, though Sienne sat watch by a small fire, studying her.

She did not look happy.

Raquel turned back to Jake, who lay completely still, his chest rising and falling with sleep.

How was it possible that he'd fallen asleep already?

She realized she was staring at him again, and she grumbled at herself as she lay down, her back to his, careful not to make any physical contact. And yet she felt him there, his space touching all of hers. She stared up at the mist, thinking on all Jake had said and all he had not.

Wondering if it was really so terrible to let the heir of the forest claim her heart after all.

JAKE WAITED until her breathing was even, until their camp had fallen quiet, and then he glanced back.

Sienne's fire had dimmed, morphing their camp into a canvas of silhouettes. He could just see Banon seated by the fire, whittling something with his knife. A cry echoed through the forest, but it was too distant to be of any concern. So far, everything seemed to be going according to plan.

Well, that wasn't entirely true. He'd never planned to have his coat ruined.

Jake looked at Raquel.

She had turned toward him in her sleep. Her features were relaxed, and her dark lashes fluttered with dreams.

Jake remembered his own.

Of *her*.

She sighed and adjusted her head, and a clump of hair slid over her face. Without thinking, Jake reached out and brushed it back, and when he tucked it behind her ear, she sighed again and leaned into his touch.

Jake's brow furrowed.

And then he pulled his hand back and turned away from her. Ignoring that strange pain in his chest.

But then her slender arm slipped around his waist, and she curled against his back.

Jake froze and nearly magicked himself out of her grasp, but then he realized her hands were like ice and she was trembling.

He could magik her another blanket. It would be easy

enough. Instead, and against his better judgment, he rolled toward her, slipped his arm beneath her head, and drew her close. Something sharp jabbed into his arm, and he grinned, realizing she'd hidden another little claw within her braid. He plucked it free from her plait and set it safely aside, then he held her until the trembling stopped, until her breathing evened.

Until he eventually fell asleep.

14

Jake had the dreams again. Of holding Raquel, of watching their children. Only this time, those children had names: Adi and Ronan. And while Ronan had the sharp features of their kith, the light stride and aristocratic air, Adi was the reflection of her mother, in body and in spirit.

And how Jake *loved* Adi.

It struck him that he should know what it was, this strange feeling that filled his chest to near bursting. This overwhelming urge to protect—that he would do *anything* to see her thrive.

Even sacrifice his own life.

Jake woke with this single thought haunting him, compounded by the warmth of the woman currently asleep in his arms.

Raquel.

It was still dark, and she slept on her side, her back to him with Jake curled around her. His arm was over her waist, holding her protectively close, as he'd done in his dream, and he breathed in her hair. It smelled of spring, of fresh flowers and tall grass and sunlight. Something he had not smelled in ages, and it stirred something deep inside of him.

No.

Jake released his hold, rolled onto his back, and closed his eyes, pressing his fingertips into them.

Fates.

He had not come all this way to be thwarted by dreams and a pair of summer-sky eyes. He hadn't lied to Raquel about the riddle. He just hadn't given her all of it:

Through blood, by blood, may your sins be paid
Spent from a mortal heart, the heir must claim.
A babe wrought by harvest's light,
And virgin be, by immortal's sight,
Who holds the only road to your salvation.

He didn't just need the affections of her heart; he also needed its *blood.*

It had been the same for Edom, though after five failed bride sacrifices, Jake and his mother had begun to wonder. Perhaps "claim" meant more than just the physical act of cutting a heart open. The Fates' meanings were so often convoluted and misunderstood.

Perhaps the heir needed to "claim" her affections as well, which was not something Edom could ever do.

So Jake's mother got an idea. Maybe Jake should try. Let her worry about transferring the birthright. But after Jake stole the last bride from his brother and hid her away at his mother's, only for her to escape into the mist and intercept a horde of Depraved, Canna endured seven more years of rot and decay. More and more of their people were added to the fallen, and King Issachar had fallen deeply ill. They did not know how much longer he would live, so if there was ever an opportunity to capitalize on this moment, to ask for the king's blessing—something he would only bestow upon Canna's successor—now was that time.

So Abecka had made the coat, Jake had formulated the sleeping draft for Edom and his men, and together, they set their new plan into motion. Besides, earning a woman's affection had always been easy for Jake. So easy, he'd made a game of it.

As he was now.

Life isn't a game, Jake. It is a gift, *coveted by those who would give anything to still have breath in their lungs—breath you and your kith take for granted.*

Jake put his hand to his chest and massaged the muscles. He couldn't understand why it ached, but then Raquel rolled toward him, nudged into his side, and murmured his name in her sleep.

Jake cursed and shoved himself to his feet. He needed some fresh air. He needed to move—*anything* but be near her right now—so he strode for Rian, who sat by the faintly glowing embers.

Hearing Jake, Rian glanced over and frowned. "You all right?"

"Fine."

Rian eyed Jake as Jake sat beside him.

Jake didn't meet his gaze. He looked to the mist instead. "Any signs of Edom?"

A beat, then Rian shook his head. "Nothing yet. I did hear a couple of Depraved about an hour ago, but nothing's come close." He paused. "What if Abecka's not there?"

Jake leaned back on his hands. He'd thought about this a lot during yesterday's travel. "Then best pray she left the thread."

Rian stared at him. "Can *you* fix it?"

"We'll find out soon enough."

Rian frowned, clearly unsatisfied. "Even if you can, do you think you'll be able to convince your father to give his blessing without her?"

Jake shrugged. "We might not have a choice. Either way, I'll find out tomorrow when I go."

Rian heard what Jake didn't say. "And what about the rest of us?"

"You're heading straight for the palace—"

"Like hell." Rian sat upright. "You can't go at this alone—"

"I won't be alone. I'll be with Raquel."

Rian gave him an annoyed look.

"The fact of the matter is that I can get there in about three hours. With the rest of you, it'll take a full day"—seeing that Rian was about to object again, Jake rested a palm upon Rian's shoulder and added—"*you know it will*, and we don't have the time. Edom is already on the move. And who knows...I might even beat you to the palace." Jake winked, but Rian was not convinced.

Rian's gaze drifted to where Raquel slept, and then he glanced sideways at Jake. "You sure you'll follow through with this?"

The question annoyed Jake, and he let it show on his face.

"I'm serious," Rian said.

"So am I." Then, "Out with it, man."

Rian sighed and rested his arms upon his knees as his gaze drifted back to her. "You're different with her."

"I'm trying to win her heart, Rian."

"Yes, but it's more than that."

"There's nothing more," Jake said. He almost believed it.

Rian appeared as though he almost did too. "She's pretty."

Jake felt a flare of defensiveness, but he smiled instead. "Makes it simple."

Rian looked at him, and then his shoulders sagged.

"Come, Rian." Jake rested a hand on Rian's shoulder. "Everything else is as we've discussed. You know this is our best chance. I wouldn't ask if it weren't necessary, but I will never get that blessing as myself."

"You could. Your father's practically blind. Just wear a fur and roll around in blood."

Jake chuckled, patted Rian's shoulder, and dropped his hand. "Unfortunately, there's the matter of everyone else who is *not* blind."

They sat quietly.

Rian dragged a hand over his face. "Fates, I hope this works, Jake. Seeing that mortal... her color... makes me remember what we lost."

Jake's gaze slid to the sleeping girl, and his chest cramped. "I know."

~

RAQUEL DREAMED OF JAKE AGAIN, but this was not the forest from before.

This one belonged to Harran.

She recognized the knobby oaks standing stubbornly between the fluffy pines—the *smell*. Of earth and rain and balsam. Somewhere, a bird chirped brightly, and a pair of vivid blue songbirds darted past, whirling and dancing around each other to welcome the spring.

And then Raquel saw herself with Jake. He stood behind her, his chin resting upon her head while his strong arms wrapped around her belly.

A belly that was swollen with child.

His child.

Somehow in Raquel's dream, within the part of her consciousness that remained distantly aware that none of this was real—*that* part stared in complete shock while her dream self lovingly regarded the two children jumping in the newly fallen leaves.

One boy, one girl.

The girl favored Raquel, the boy Jake.

The boy possessed Jake's easy grace and lightness even as he ran around, wielding his trusty stick as he attacked invisible foes. He darted around them and then jumped onto Jake's back with a battle cry.

Jake released Raquel and feigned surprise and terror like any adoring father, letting his little cub have every advantage. Giving just enough resistance to prolong the fight, to build the boy's endurance, and to help him believe that there was nothing he could not overcome.

The two wrestled and rolled, the little girl joined in, Jake laughed heartily, and Raquel's heart felt too big for her chest.

And then the forest and children were gone, replaced by a bedchamber Raquel did not know. Like the forest, it was a place that belonged in Harran, with its wooden walls and thatched ceiling, the small wood stove and humble furnishings.

But Raquel wasn't alone.

Jake was there, the two of them standing before the glowing hearth. He wore only breeches, and she a nightdress that draped from one shoulder, the fabric so thin she could see her slender silhouette through the material. His arms slid around her waist, and the inked vines around his biceps flexed as he pulled her against him and crushed his lips to hers. *Claiming.*

Raquel could not look away. She was somehow inside the moment and outside of it. Watching the way he held her, kissed her—knowing it wasn't really happening—but also feeling every pulse of his lips as he crashed into her and drew back like the tide. As the heat of his skin burned through her thin slip, as his callused palms slowly slid beneath her hem.

Raquel knew this was a dream. That she should not want this like the Raquel in her dream so obviously did.

And yet she could not bring herself to stop it.

She could not bring herself to wake up.

His lips were like wine, his touch fire, and Raquel wanted to feel those flames all over her body. And so Raquel let her semi-consciousness drift into this moment, giving herself to it completely so that she and Dream Raquel were one and the same.

So that she could pretend—just for a moment—that this beautiful moment was real.

And when Jake lifted her gown, Raquel did not stop him. She helped him, eager to get it off. To feel his skin flush with hers, to feel his lips everywhere. He tossed her gown aside, but rather than pull her down with him, he drew back, grabbed her face tenderly between his hands, and gazed into her eyes.

His eyes were liquid gold. "I love you," he said, and then, once he was certain she heard him—that she *believed* him—he lowered his mouth to hers.

Of course, that was when Raquel awoke.

She had been so startled by those words and his confession that she had completely forgotten to hold on to the dream. It had slipped right through her fingers and moved on to finish in a plane Raquel would never see or experience.

And how she wanted to.

That truth startled her more than any other.

Raquel opened her eyes. It wasn't quite morning, but the

mist had lightened, and she glanced over to where she'd last seen Jake. He was gone, the blankets still rumpled where he had lain, and Raquel couldn't stop the prick of disappointment she felt at his absence.

I love you.

The words echoed in her mind and heart.

Raquel rubbed her eyes and groaned. She was supposed to be contriving a plan to protect Harran from ever having to sacrifice a bride again, not having (highly inappropriate!) dreams about her captor. Maybe the mist was altering her mind, or perhaps there was still a bit of Depraved poison in her blood that Sienne had missed. Whatever the reason, something had to be wrong, because Raquel's dreams never lied. They were always rooted in truth, though they might exaggerate, but Jake would never—not in a thousand, wasted years—say *I love you*.

"Good, you're awake."

Raquel froze, then very slowly, she lowered her hands and opened her eyes.

Jake stood over her, illuminated from behind by what remained of a fire. She was *very* concerned that she hadn't heard him approach.

"Get up," he said, his tone stiff. Not at all the way he'd spoken to her in her dream. "It's time to go."

He snapped his fingers, and her blanket vanished.

Raquel sat up with a start, but Jake was already walking away toward Vizzi.

"So much for manners," Raquel murmured to herself as she stood and dusted her skirts.

"*Scoundrel*," he said over his shoulder while pointing to himself, and Raquel grumbled as she started after him.

Most of the camp still slept, though a few were beginning to stir. Sienne sat beside the fire, drinking out of a water pouch, but when she lowered it, her gaze met Raquel's, and she looked promptly back to the flames.

Meanwhile, Raquel was careful not to step on anyone sleeping, and when she reached Jake, she asked, "What about the others?"

Jake placed his neatly folded coat into one of Vizzi's bags, and he didn't look over. "We'll join them later."

"Where are we going?"

"To my mother's."

Something had changed since last night. Raquel did not know how, being that she'd been sleeping, and she couldn't quite put a finger on it, but he was definitely acting different this morning. Irritable and withdrawn and...was he intentionally keeping physical distance from her?

Raquel took a few steps toward him, and he *conveniently* took a few steps away, though his attention remained on Vizzi.

"I thought you didn't know where she was," Raquel asked, deciding she didn't much like this Jake. She missed the other one, infuriating though he was.

Jake pulled the flap over the bag's opening and tied it shut. "I don't. We're going to her private residence."

Raquel frowned. "She doesn't live with your father?"

Jake chuckled and moved around to Vizzi's other side. "No."

"Why do you laugh?"

Jake ran his hand over Vizzi's side and checked the saddle's straps. "If you knew my father, you'd understand."

Raquel thought of her own mother and father before her mother had died. They had loved one another very much, and her death had nearly destroyed her father. In many ways, it had. "What a sad marriage," she said.

"It is a contract to secure peace—nothing more. Certainly, *my bride* can relate." Jake threw a pointed look at her over his saddle, and Raquel decided she also didn't like his assessment of marriage.

He returned his attention to Vizzi. "And anyway, how *sad* can it be? My mother is the queen of Canna, and she has access to every provision this kingdom has to offer. Your mortal ideals of love could never make such claim."

Raquel thought of her parents' love again and also her dream. "I would take a simple life with a love that could move mountains over an empty marriage with all the riches and power in the world."

Jake looked at her. It was the first time he had *really* looked at her since he'd woken her this morning, and Raquel's cheeks warmed from the pure intensity of it. "You are such a contradiction," he said at last.

That heat crept down her neck. "I'm not sure what you're talking about."

He stepped around Vizzi and stopped before her—*right* before her. As close as he could possibly be without actually touching her, and she felt every inch of space between them. "You speak of love that moves mountains, and yet you tried to murder your betrothed in his sleep," he said lowly, his words a brush of warmth against her lips, but before Raquel could find her voice, Jake held out a hand and said, with a triumphant twist of his lips, "Left leg."

Raquel gasped in outrage.

"Come now," Jake said. "I don't fancy getting stabbed while we ride today."

Raquel grumbled as she lifted the left side of her skirts and unhooked the blade there. Jake's eyes were on hers the entire time, but she didn't shy away. No, she stared right back, as if parrying his blade in this new unspoken battle between them—a war of motivation and opposing desire—and she set the dagger into his open palm with gusto, then let her skirts slowly slide back into position.

His brow raised as he palmed the dagger then leaned in close, his mouth at her ear. "And the one in your corset," he whispered so softly.

Raquel's her heart pounded, and she felt simultaneously furious and undone from his proximity. Still, she did not shy away as she reached behind herself and slid the slender file from a rib in her corset and set it in his open palm.

"Satisfied, my prince?" she said, her voice a breath.

He lingered there, his mouth still at her ear. "Almost." His voice was velvet, and a hundred butterflies fluttered inside of her. "Now, if you wouldn't mind..." He gestured at the saddle with her blade. When she didn't move, he added, "Or I shall be forced to pick you up and toss..."

Raquel gathered her skirts and climbed into the saddle. Well, truthfully, she was so flustered that she missed her footing and fell *against* the saddle. Jake started to reach for her, but she resolutely grabbed the horn and pulled herself up, shoving him back a little as she did.

Jake chuckled again, climbed on after, slid one arm around her waist, and pulled her back to his chest.

Raquel told herself it wasn't the most glorious feeling in the world.

"If we're not there by midday, head back to Little Mignon," Jake said to Sienne, who nodded, though her gaze narrowed on them as Jake nudged Vizzi onward, into the mist.

15

Try as she might, Raquel could not shake her dreams. It didn't help that she shared a saddle with Jake, who kept one arm secured around her waist, his hard chest pressed to her back. Her mind kept reverting to those moments in the dream woods, the way he'd kissed her, and the look in his eyes when he'd said *I love you*.

Those three little words taunted her with every mile, teasing her with beautiful possibility while her rational self struggled to hold fast to reality. Jake didn't have a heart. He could *not* love. He was only "courting" her because his curse demanded he lay claim to her affections. Not at all from his own volition. It really was just a game for him—*she* was a game, one he needed to win.

The problem was that a large and quickly growing part of her *wanted* him to win. It wanted him to court her as Dream Jake would have done, and it persisted that his motivation was more than just this game. That he actually felt something for her beyond triumph.

But soon after they left the others, Jake fell back into silence, and the sound of Vizzi's gallop served as their only conversation. It rumbled like Raquel's heart, these erratic beats and pounding rhythms, full of questions and yearnings she could neither allay nor understand.

Until she could no longer bear it.

And when Jake slowed Vizzi to a walk, Raquel said, "Is there something wrong, Highness?"

She swayed with him in the saddle.

"I don't know, is there?" His tone teased, but a brusque undercurrent clipped his words.

Raquel stole a glance back at him. His shrewd gaze fixed immutably ahead, his kith features as sharp as steel. He was all purpose, all drive and fierce determination—a man riding hard for the attainment of his goal.

"You're uncharacteristically quiet," Raquel said.

"I'm focused on the path ahead. In case you hadn't noticed, it's just you and me"—Vizzi snorted, and Jake patted Vizzi's haunches—"and dear old Vizzi; of course I would never forget you, boy...but I would prefer we *not* be caught unaware by a horde of Depraved. Stubborn as you are, my bride, not even you would survive another infection."

Raquel considered him. "It's more than that."

He eyed her, one brow raised. "What is it about you that persists in seeing more where there is none?"

"There is more. That's why you drown yourself in wine —to numb all the feelings you say you don't have."

Jake's gaze narrowed and slid back to the trees. "You really need to—"

"You say life's a game." She cut him off. "That it's simply a series of wins and losses, but I don't believe you. Not for a second."

"That is your burden. Not mine."

"Fair," she clipped. "I imagine it's difficult to carry one

more burden when you're already carrying the loss of tens of thousands."

Jake's arm flinched, his jaw flexed, and his gaze snapped right back to her, where it burned. Raquel didn't know what had prompted her to poke and prod at the open wounds Jake fought so desperately to hide—open wounds he refused to admit were even there—but she was angry and tired, and she was so tired of playing his little games.

Especially when it came to her heart.

"Careful, my bride," Jake warned, that kith wildness in his eyes. "You speak of things you do not know."

"*Then tell me.*"

His expression shifted—softened, almost, as his gaze drifted to her lips, and then he said, "Has anyone ever mentioned that you are beautiful when you're angry?"

"This isn't a game, Jake!"

He smiled viciously and leaned in close. His breath brushed her cheek, and his arm tightened possessively around her waist. "Isn't it?"

"I do not play games with hearts," Raquel said through her teeth. "And I will not let you play games with mine."

He looked at her as she looked at him, that invisible war between them. That clash of intent.

Jake frowned. "Pity," he said at last, and then he looked ahead, loosened his grip, and leaned away from her.

And Raquel felt a hot spark of anger. "That's it, then? I really am just a game for you? You're really that callous and unfeeling?"

"No heart, remember?" he said, tone dry. "In fact, *you're* the one who accused me of it."

"Well, I've changed my mind."

Jake laughed.

Raquel didn't appreciate it, and it only made her more persistent. "I *know* you have a heart."

"Do you, now? How convenient..."

It was an overwhelming surge of anger and defensiveness that prompted her to say, "I saw your heart. In my dreams."

As soon as the words left her lips, Raquel couldn't believe she'd admitted it. The only ones who knew about her dreams were Lee and her father. She'd been too afraid to tell anyone else, and they certainly hadn't wanted the elders to know. No telling how they might have used her. But now that she'd said the words, Raquel suddenly found herself *wanting* to tell Jake. To see if her dreams would strike a chord within him and unearth the Jake that Dream Raquel wanted so badly to be real.

"You dreamed about me, my bride?" Jake drawled.

"I dreamed of the stag," she continued slowly. "Exactly as it was, but Banon was not there. It was just you."

Jake snorted. "And I suppose next you'll tell me how you saw me riding with you through this forest—"

"I saw your brother, too. I saw him cut a switch and whip you with it—he was so much bigger than you when you were little—and then I saw you run into the woods, tending to all the animals that he abused for sport..."

Jake had drawn Vizzi to an abrupt halt.

"Who told you this?" His voice was low and dangerous. He was not playing around anymore.

"No one told me anything. As I said: they were dreams."

"Don't lie to me."

She looked back at him. Their gazes collided like crossed blades. "I am not lying, Highness, and I don't play games. It is the truth."

He studied her, his expression inscrutable. "Do you often dream?"

"More often than I would like."

He searched her as if he could find the lie hidden somewhere in her expression. "Is it always of the things that have transpired?"

"Not always," she answered. "Sometimes it is the future I see."

His gaze penetrated. "Have you seen my future?"

Raquel's lips parted, but she hesitated. Did she tell him what she had seen of them? Of their children?

Jake grabbed her face between his hands, and Raquel froze, instantly transported back to her dream, but the look in *this* Jake's eyes was not loving. It was deadly and furious and serious, and maybe even a little afraid. "*What have you seen*?"

Raquel swallowed, caught between his large hands. Caught between dream and reality. "I…don't know."

"What do you mean *you don't know*?"

"I mean that what I've seen doesn't make any sense."

Jake's gaze bored into hers as if he might stare the truth out. "Explain."

"I saw…us."

His brow furrowed, his grip softened, and he leaned back a fraction, wary. "What were we doing?" His tone had turned cautious.

Raquel felt her cheeks flame, but she pressed on. "Watching our children. A girl and a boy. The boy looked just like you, but the girl favored me, and we…"

Jake dropped his hands and turned his face away. "Utterly preposterous."

The words hurt. Raquel wasn't expecting them to. "You asked. I'm just telling you what I saw."

Jake sat still and quiet. He still hadn't urged Vizzi to walk, and Vizzi snorted with restlessness. "Who else knows about this…unique little gift of yours?"

"My father and my brother, Lee."

"Yes, I imagine they wouldn't want that groveling little

weasel Hamarr knowing anything about your little gift, would they?" Jake murmured to himself, and then—to her surprise—he dismounted.

His boots landed upon dried leaves with a crunch. "We're here."

Raquel blinked, surprised, and it took her a moment to adjust from their tense conversation to the landscape immediately surrounding them.

Raquel saw nothing that resembled a private dwelling, not until Jake began walking, and then she slowly made sense of a structure in the mist. Straight lines for walls, and a flat rooftop to close them in. Not much of a dwelling from what she could tell. She jumped down from Vizzi, then followed after Jake, and as she neared the structure, she realized that the mist hadn't obscured anything at all. It *was* just a tall and simple box made of old, knotted wood that was slowly being reclaimed by the forest.

"What is this, a privy?" Raquel asked, more to herself.

She thought she heard Jake chuckle.

"No, it's my mother's," he said, then opened the door and ducked through.

16

"Fine. Leave me out here with your monsters and bleeding trees," Raquel mumbled, then walked through the door after Jake and froze.

She was inside of an atrium of sorts—a mesmerizing arid space that let in light from above, with arched doorways and windows, all open to fresh air. Similar to the outpost, there was no mist in this place. Here was an enchanting garden of *living* plants—thick vines and palms and ferns—all of them draped in flowers.

In *color*.

So this was where Jake had found the rose.

Raquel had never seen such vibrant hues, and she immediately thought of Harran's stories. The one's she'd grown up with, but even they failed to do this justice. Deep green vines as thick as her arms festooned from the ceiling, all of which were covered in an exotic assortment of flowers so saturated with color they practically dripped with it. More flower petals tumbled across the mosaic floor, pushed by a breeze Raquel had not felt outside, and on that breeze, she smelled the sweetest fragrance. Like honeysuckle and jasmine and fresh rain. Water trickled from a fountain at the center, which was where Raquel's attention fixed.

The fountain was composed of three bowls—three tiers—and rising through them at its center were the figures of a man and a woman, both covered in rose petals. His hair fell to his chin, and hers cascaded over her body, covering her nakedness. They stood close, facing one another with their waists touching, and the man held the woman's face in his hands as he gazed lovingly down upon her, their lips a fraction apart.

The dream flashed in her mind again. Jake's hands on her face, the look in his eyes when he said *I love you.*

"It was a gift for my mother on her wedding day," Jake said suddenly, startling her.

He had stopped beside her, but his attention remained on the fountain.

"It seems a cruel thing to keep, considering what you said about their marriage," Raquel said.

Jake didn't answer immediately. "I doubt she thought of that at all. She's always been a preserver of rare artifacts." Jake turned away to appraise the room, and a mark of sadness furrowed his brow and turned those golden eyes as dark as sap.

"Your kingdom was like this once," Raquel said.

"Yes," he said, and then he walked on. Purpose lent power to his stride and hardened his gaze, and he stopped behind a desk buried in thick tomes and parchment.

Raquel reached up and touched one of the little roses blooming off the vine. It was so fragrant, so vivid in color, and its petals were like silk between her fingers. "How did this survive?"

Jake opened a drawer, closed it. "My mother. She fashioned this place as a sanctuary, a hidden respite, if you will—she was always so fond of nature."

His tone was softer when he spoke of his mother, Raquel noticed. Another glimmer of the Jake from her dreams.

"You inherited that from her," Raquel said.

Jake glanced up from the desk and arched a brow at her. "There are no secrets when one dreams as you do."

"I fear a lifetime of dreams would not reveal all of yours."

His forehead creased, and he turned his attention back to the desk.

And then Raquel resumed walking, taking in all that Jake's mother had saved. The variety of color and flowers and potted grasses. "So her magik protected this place from the curse?" Raquel trailed her fingers over the soft fronds of a palm.

"Yes," he replied, now turned to a shelf, where he rummaged through vases and jars. "But the curse still seeps inside. It comes to claim all of us eventually."

"Claims you *how*?" Raquel asked.

Jake picked up a box and absently traced his fingertip over a symbol along the lid. "It is like a disease. We breathe it in, and we rot away from the inside out."

"You become Depraved."

A muscle ticked in his jaw, and a sardonic smile curled his lips. "It seems you are right about me, after all. I did have a heart once, but it has rotted."

"I don't believe you."

He laughed, but the sound was dark.

Raquel took a step toward him. "I'm serious."

He stopped laughing and looked straight at her. "So am I."

Raquel took his statement as a direct challenge, and she approached the desk, persuaded by forces and feelings she did not quite understand. Perhaps she was simply weary of this game, of this war between them—the war within *herself*

—and she needed to quiet that persistent whisper once and for all.

Or make it sing.

Jake's gaze narrowed, and he stood perfectly, inhumanly still as she rounded the desk. In fact, he didn't seem to breathe. She stopped before him, close enough that if she stood on her toes and tipped her chin, their lips would touch, but she did not. She simply stood there glaring at him, as if to stare out Dream Jake once and for all.

"And you're a liar," she said.

His eyes were huge and dark as they stared into hers. "I cannot lie, my bride."

"You have lied so well and for so long that you can't even recognize truth anymore."

He frowned, and his gaze moved between her eyes. "It's your dream, isn't it? It's making you persist in seeing things that are not there."

Raquel had the strangest suspicion that those words weren't just for her, but that they were for him too. "Then kiss me," she said in that slip of space between them.

Jake stilled. Everything about him stilled as he continued to stare at her. Desire suddenly flared in his eyes, and his gaze flickered to her lips. "I thought you would not bargain for kisses." His words were a feather upon her lips.

"This is no bargain, my prince." She tipped her face closer, and his eyes devoured her. "Kiss me, and tell me you feel nothing. Hold my face in your hands, look into my eyes, and tell me that you could never love—"

Jake crushed his mouth to hers, stopping her words.

Raquel was shocked at first, but then Jake moved his now-free hand to her chin and cupped it as he kissed her back against the desk.

And Raquel felt her heart melting.

If she'd been enchanted by his kiss in her dream, it was

nothing compared to the real thing. Nothing compared to the real hunger in his lips, the way they took and gave and clung, and her dreams did not come close to capturing the soft warmth of his tongue as it pushed into her mouth, searching and coaxing. Drawing her out, drawing her to him. His breath had tasted sweet in her dream, and it tasted sweet now, but there was a fever in it that her dream could never bring—a heat that spread a very real fire through her belly and tingled down her legs, and her body arched into his on its own accord, and Jake moaned against her mouth.

"Tell me I mean nothing to you," she said against his lips. "That this is just a game."

Jake tried to kiss her again, but she tilted her head back further and looked into his dark and ravenous eyes.

"*Tell me*," she persisted.

A half groan, half growl sounded deep in his throat, and in answer, he let go of her wrists, slid his arm around her waist, and pulled her tight against his own body as his lips claimed hers again.

This time, Raquel couldn't bring herself to interrupt him, and for a split second, her senses flickered between present and dream. Between the real and current *now* and those moments she had seen in her sleep, with the two of them before the fire. They were completely separate moments, yet they were the same, simultaneously then and now, both planes playing out together, but apart. Amplified, almost, because of it.

And now that Raquel's hands were free, she let them search. She combed through his dark and gloriously thick hair that was even silkier than she'd imagined, and then she slid her palms down his back, feeling the muscles tense and shift as he held her, kissed her. He grabbed her waist, lifted and set her firmly upon the desk, then pushed himself closer, into the fabric of her skirts so that he was standing between her legs, and he kissed her deeply.

Raquel knew that she was falling down a well she could never climb out of if she didn't stop this now.

Especially as his hands squeezed down her legs and slipped beneath her skirts, lifting them higher.

And higher.

Raquel grabbed his hands and held them firmly, stopping him, her heart near exploding in her chest. "Tell me you feel nothing, my prince," she demanded.

Jake dragged his lips from her neck and gazed up at her. His pupils were huge, his breath quick, but he did not speak.

"You say you cannot lie, so tell me that *I* am just a game for you." She squeezed his hands and brought them to her breast. "That this is nothing but a temporary win amidst a long game of losses. Tell me we have no future, that there is no family. That this is nothing more than a simple diversion to pass your time."

Jake didn't move, didn't seem to breathe. His lips parted, and then someone started clapping.

Raquel and Jake both turned their heads to the sound, where a bear of a man stood just inside the doorway, surrounded by dozens of armed Forest kith. It was Prince Edom—the *real* Prince Edom—and though she had never laid eyes on him, she knew it was him because he looked *exactly* how Jake had appeared while wearing that glamoured cape. In that look—in that one prolonged glance—she knew that even if Jake were wearing the glamoured coat and standing right beside his brother, she would know them apart. If she had thought Jake callous and unfeeling, it paled in comparison to the cold emptiness in Edom's black gaze. He truly was a brute, a wild animal in human form, driven by cold purpose and an insatiable hunger for power.

It was little wonder Jake and his mother had lost faith in Edom's ability to break the curse.

This was the man from her dreams who had pushed Jake away from the palace. The one who had tortured animals for sport and left them to die.

The one she needed to kill.

And he was smiling cruelly. "Well, well, well, I do believe you've rendered my traitorous little brother speechless."

17

"Edom," Jake said. There was nothing kind in Jake's voice. He slid Raquel from the desk, set her back upon the floor, and took three steps toward Prince Edom, only to find himself blocked by the points of half a dozen swords.

And Jake smiled viciously. "Good evening, gentlemen. Still defending my dear brother's insecurities, I see."

Edom took a step, then another, each footfall landing like a brick upon the mosaic tiles. "And you are still slinking in the shadows like the traitorous little worm you are. Did you really think you would get away with this?"

"Where is she, Edom?" Jake's voice was dark, his expression murderous.

"Somewhere she can no longer interfere." Edom reached up and plucked a blood-red rose from the vine. "I'll be honest. I could not believe that my own mother would favor one son *so much* that she would act against the other. Not until I saw the rose upon that stag. Then I knew." Those last words ground out between his teeth, and he crushed the little bloom in his fist and watched those petals fall as they disintegrated into ash.

"If you so much as laid a finger on her, so help me—" Jake pitched forward, but those sword points remained resolute.

Edom moved between his men and their swords and stopped before Jake. "You'll *what*? There is nothing you can do. I have three elite and fifty men standing outside. I expected you would hear our approach, but it makes sense now. You were"—his gaze slid to Raquel—"otherwise engaged. Tell me, when, exactly, were you planning to kill her? While making love to her, or after?" Edom must have seen something in Raquel's face, because his eyes suddenly glittered with cruel delight, and he added, "He didn't tell you?"

Raquel looked at Jake, and her heart pounded. "Is this true?"

Jake did not answer, and he did not meet her gaze.

Edom, however, looked positively ecstatic. "Why, yes. He needs your blood. From your heart."

But Jake still wasn't looking at her—*would not* look at her. His attention fixed only on Edom, and her legs began to tremble in fear. In deep disappointment. "Answer me, Jake... *is this true*?" Raquel demanded.

It was then that Jake's gaze slid to hers, but it was not her Jake that looked at her now. Not the man from her dreams or the one she'd come to know. This Jake's smile was mirthless, and his eyes shone with cruelty as his lips curled in mockery of her misplaced hope. "As true as your mortality."

His words were a boulder to her chest. "You said you had to claim my heart...that was your riddle. So you lied—"

"You told her the riddle?" Edom looked to Jake, surprised.

"I did," Jake drawled. "Just not all of it."

A beat.

"'*Through blood, by blood, may your sins be paid, spent from a mortal heart, the heir must claim,*'" Jake said.

His words were a knife through Raquel's chest. He was right; he hadn't lied—not exactly. He'd simply left out the first line, but it was the most important line of all, for by it, the rest hinged.

Starting with blood from her mortal heart.

"So this was all just a game to you." Raquel's voice trembled. Her entire body trembled. "You really *are* a heartless, selfish..." There were so many names she wanted to call him, but her breaking heart bled all over her words. "It was all a lie."

"I never lied, my bride," Jake answered simply. "You just refused to believe me."

"Oh, no...let it be known that Jakobián *is* a liar. He speaks in lies. He is such a master of twisting truth that not even our curse can prevent his lies completely. He always... finds an edge." Edom tilted his head, and his gaze razed over Raquel in a way that Raquel found extremely impolite. "I see why you fought so hard for this one. She is an unusually pretty little mortal, isn't she?"

"And her heart is claimed, so what now, brother?" Jake taunted.

Edom took a small step closer to Jake. "Claimed? I think not. It is broken. And besides. The dead cannot claim anything." And Edom slung his fist at Jake's face.

Raquel gasped, and her hands flew to her mouth as the force of Edom's strike sent Jake reeling. Blood trickled from Jake's nose, and the skin around his eye bloomed an angry red, but he was...*smiling*.

"Seems I struck a nerve." Jake wiped the blood from his nose with the back of his hand.

"Kill him," Edom said darkly.

An uncertain second passed as Edom's guards deliberated between the command of one prince and the abject treachery toward another. But in that split second, Jake looked at Raquel, smiled brilliantly, and vanished.

Completely and utterly vanished. He winked out of existence, just like his sword.

Edom stuttered and spat, and his expression bloated with rage. "Come out and fight, you coward!"

But Edom's words were met with silence, and while Edom and his guard searched the room for signs of Jake, Raquel found herself searching too. For certainly he would not have abandoned her now to this actual bear of a man.

And yet...why shouldn't he?

He'd been planning to kill her all along. He was *not* the man from her dreams. The real Jake could not feel affection. The real Jake knew only self-preservation. If Jake felt love at all, it was only for self.

And he was right; he'd lied about none of it. It *had* been all a game to him, and she was nothing more than a prize.

Edom's attention settled back upon her. "Bind the girl, and put her on my horse. We leave now."

18

Raquel's jaw ached from the gag. They'd been traveling for hours. How many hours, Raquel had no idea. There was no sun to gauge time because the mist hid all.

Prince Edom kept them riding at a steady pace, stopping occasionally to observe the way forward while sometimes consulting one of his guards. But then the branches would come alive, reaching for them as they'd reached for Jake's party, though they were much bolder than they'd ever been with Jake. Edom spoke a word, as Jake had done, and the branches did retreat, but hesitantly. When Edom spoke, his command felt more like an inconvenience, and the trees never retreated completely. Raquel had the distinct impression that Edom could not navigate the mist as easily as Jake, but whatever his particular inhibition, the time labored on.

Especially because she could not get Jake's words out of her head: *I never lied, my bride. You simply refused to believe me.*

But then she would remember their kiss. Their real, actual kiss, and she could not believe it was all for show—

that he truly felt nothing. That his only intention was to kill her in her distraction. Except he'd also vanished and left her with this brute.

Still, she kept searching for Jake. She also couldn't believe he'd risk his position for the throne by capturing her only to vanish the moment Edom appeared. A liar and a traitor—yes, he was both of those things. But a coward? Raquel did not think so. He'd planned this coup for saints knew how long; he would not give up without a fight.

Life is a game, he had said. He would wait. He would wait until the game favored his odds.

Eventually, it became too dark to see, and Edom—with the aid of his kith—set up camp amidst a cluster of enormous and bloated roots. They forged a perimeter the way Jake and his men had done, but there was no blanket for Raquel this time. Edom dumped her right upon the earth and said, "How's that for a marriage bed, my bride?"

A few of his kith chuckled.

Raquel, who had managed to work off her gag, spat at his feet.

Edom crouched, grabbed a fistful of her hair, and jerked her close, nearly nose to nose. "Do not think that because I need your heart that I will not harm your body."

Raquel could not look at him without seeing all the horrors he'd committed in her dreams. "You are no better than the Depraved you fear," she growled.

Edom's eyes narrowed. "And you are a fool. You actually believed my brother felt anything for you."

"I know he does." She said it to get under Edom's skin. She said it in case Jake was somewhere near, listening. She said it because she still wanted so badly to believe it.

Edom gripped her hair so hard she winced. "Foolish girl. You felt what he wanted you to feel. You believed what he wanted you to believe. Jakobián is a liar and a cheat."

"And you are a monster."

He released her hair and struck her across the face hard enough that she fell to the ground. She didn't have hands to stop her fall; they were bound. And then her view was of Edom's heavy black boots. He bent over her and spit upon her face. Raquel flinched as the spittle trailed down her cheek.

"Mortal filth," he snarled. "Gag her," he ordered and stomped off.

Two of his kith came forward immediately and refastened the gag. Raquel winced as they caught some of her hair in it, but she did not cry out. She lay there, glaring as they walked away laughing. As that bear of a man talked and drank with his kith. At one point, Prince Edom caught her gaze and smiled viciously.

"Do you have eyes for your betrothed, my bride?" he taunted. "Eager to consummate our marriage? I can make arrangements for that now if you like."

Raquel turned her glare to the trees instead, and a few of his kith chuckled. He murmured something to his men that Raquel did not hear, but he did not get up from his seat.

Where was Jake?

The more time that passed and he did not reappear, the more Raquel began to wonder if she was mistaken about him, after all.

She didn't expect to fall asleep, but then her eyes snapped open and her back ached where a rock dug into it, and when she glanced over, she noticed the fire was gone and the mist had lightened.

She'd also dreamed of Jake again.

Holding her, kissing her. Such love in his eyes as he whispered upon her lips, "I love you."

That whisper echoed even now like a torment as her body rose to consciousness, and *Almighty in heaven*, if it hadn't felt so real. It made her chest ache, experiencing something so beautiful—this love that could move mountains.

To know that it was not real.

She heard movement and glanced back to see Edom urinating on glowing embers, and she promptly glanced away.

Edom snickered.

And then he was hoisting her up to her feet, holding her before him firmly by the shoulders.

"Don't worry," Edom said. "You'll get used to it soon enough."

The idea made Raquel want to vomit, and she would have said as much except for the gag still tied resolutely around her mouth. So instead, she glared.

Edom leaned closer. "If we weren't in such a hurry, I'd make you get used to it right now."

A hungry breeze pushed at her, and branches snapped and creaked. Edom's attention shot to the trees. "Time to go, boys," he said, then tossed her onto the horse, and within two minutes, they were all mounted and riding again through the mist and trees.

Into the unknown.

JAKE FOLLOWED, never too close but never too far. Always with Raquel just in his sight.

Last night had been...difficult.

He'd fallen asleep to the memories of that kiss—their real, actual kiss—further compounded by the ones from his dreams, and when his eyes snapped open, his chest ached worse than before. As if something were being ripped out of it.

No...

As if something were growing *inside* of it, tearing through muscle and cartilage and bone to make way for itself.

However, this time he found himself less concerned with the why of it and more concerned for her.

Raquel.

He'd nearly revealed himself the moment Edom had grabbed her hair. Never in all his life had he felt so fiercely protective over anyone—aside from himself. It was the same feeling he'd had in his dreams, and it took everything inside of him to hold back. To wait. To be patient as the game unfolded so that he might strike when the odds favored him most. It was the only way to deal with Edom, and Jake had perfected it after over so many years.

And yet he'd nearly winked back into existence the second Edom had touched her.

You actually believed my brother felt anything for you. Edom had said.

I know he does.

Jake could not get those words out of his mind. The conviction in her voice. The look in her eyes when she had gazed *directly at him*, which was impossible because there was no way she could have seen him upon that high tree branch. But those eyes had locked on his and skewered him to the core, and Jake had found himself wondering if this mortal possessed magik after all.

But then Edom had stormed off, sparing Jake from acting rashly, and Raquel had fallen asleep against the tree root, though he'd watched her stubbornly fight fatigue. She'd lasted impressively late into the night, but her mortal body had finally succumbed, and her consciousness had drifted.

She turned in her sleep and muttered something he

could not make out, not with that blasted gag, but he wondered if she'd been dreaming about him.

He'd seen her reach subconsciously for a rib at her corset, where she—undoubtedly—kept another one of her little claws. Edom hadn't noticed. None of them had. All too inflated with their own superiority to ever be concerned over a mortal. She hadn't reached for that little weapon once today, but of course she wasn't fool enough to try to take on Edom and all his kith alone.

She did not realize that she wouldn't be alone.

It wasn't until Edom had fallen asleep that Jake finally relaxed, and so he'd settled back against a tree branch, legs extended and ankles crossed, with Raquel directly in his sight. He eventually fell asleep only for her to be the subject of his dreams—again—and they were much more vivid this time. He blamed their *actual* kiss for that.

Fates, that kiss.

It had simultaneously ripped him apart and sewn him back together.

When dawn arrived, he'd watched the girl rise to consciousness, watched his brother grab her arms and pull her to her feet and hold on to her. It took every ounce of Jake's willpower not to manifest. The wind was the best he could do, but thankfully it had worked and set Edom firmly upon his goal.

So they continued, keeping this irritatingly slow pace through the wood while Jake followed behind. The occasional cry of a Depraved echoed through the mist, but they never drew nearer, and Jake wondered what Edom had done to keep them so preoccupied.

No, Jake feared what Edom had done.

Again, Edom stopped at nightfall. Again, they situated Raquel. Again, Jake watched from a high branch until she fell asleep upon her side; however, her features did not relax in sleep, and her body shuddered with cold.

Jake looked to Edom, who had passed out with drink. Two of his guards sat watch, gazing in opposite directions.

Worthless.

Jake slid down from his perch and crept into their camp, his footfalls silent upon the soft earth. He walked right past one of the guards on watch, invisible due to his glamour. The guard, however, sat upright, and one hand went to his sword on reflex as he scanned their surroundings. But he did not see Jake—could not. He merely sensed what his eyes could not see.

And Jake waited.

He waited until the guard's posture relaxed, and then Jake crept on.

To Raquel.

He knelt behind her, close but not touching. Hesitant to touch, but also feeling this overwhelming urge to be nearer to her. Jake crouched there, deliberating. Somehow he knew that if he crossed this boundary, he would never come back.

Except.

He had the distinct impression he had already crossed. Because it had nearly killed him to see the look on her face when she had realized it had all been a lie.

You have lied so well and for so long that you can't even recognize truth anymore.

Another shudder rolled through Raquel's body, and that decided him. Quietly, carefully, he lay down behind her, slid his arm around her waist and drew her back against him. Her body relaxed against him, into his warmth.

He remembered his dream, and he glanced down to where her belly had been full and rounded with child.

Raquel sighed, rolled into him, and buried her face in his chest.

Something cracked inside Jake's own.

His hand slid up her back and into her hair—such soft and luxurious hair—where the cloth was tied. He worked quickly and slipped the tie free, then tucked the gag into his pocket, untied her wrists, and tossed that rope aside.

"Please don't leave, Jake," she murmured against his chest.

Jake's chest tightened, and he drew her closer. "You do not know what you ask of me," he whispered so softly, and then he wondered if, perhaps, she did.

19

Raquel first noticed the kiss of cold. She'd been unusually warm and comfortable, and then suddenly she was not. The warmth had pulled away and left a seeping chill behind, and Raquel opened her eyes.

Her first thought was of Jake.

She'd dreamed of him again, and yet she could have sworn it was real. That he'd untied her gag, that his arms had slid around her waist, that he'd breathed into her hair and whispered words she could not recall. She could still smell the sweet scent of spring that seemed to cling to his clothes, and she could still feel the weight of his embrace, heavy and comforting, just as she could acutely feel the absence of it.

She didn't know why her heart persisted in this—in its feelings for him—or why it had latched so desperately and defiantly onto a dream.

Except.

He had kissed her. That part, at least, had not been a dream. It had been real and sweet and as brilliant as the dawn, and it had set a sun inside of her that would not dim.

I never lied, my bride. You simply refused to believe me.

Raquel sighed and...

Froze.

She could sigh.

Her hands flew to her mouth where the gag...

Her hands were free.

How was this possible?

Raquel flexed her jaw, and she was staring at her unbound hands when a pair of heavy boots appeared before her. She followed those heavy boots with her eyes, up a pair of wide calves, and over a broad and hairy build until her gaze met Prince Edom's.

"Where are your ties?" He growled like a bear as he searched the ground, and then he grabbed her hands and jerked her to her feet. "*Where are her damned ties*?" he shouted at his men, who now scrambled like ants having their anthill destroyed.

"What did you do with them?" Edom jerked her closer and bent in her face. Raquel was too bewildered to respond. "Did you cut your way out?"

"No, I—"

"Are you hiding a blade from me, mortal?" Edom snapped, and now his eyes raked over her frame. "I will strip you down until I uncover every last—"

"Found it," said one of his guards, approaching them, rope in hand.

The rope was clearly uncut, and Edom let out a puff of a breath. He grabbed the rope, jerked Raquel's hands forward, and tied her wrists again.

"The gag?" Edom barked.

"I couldn't find it, your grace," the guard replied. "But this will work."

A beat, and then Edom was shoving a new piece of fabric into her mouth that tasted like mildew. Two minutes later, his guards threw her back upon the horse, Edom glared at the mist, mumbling something beneath Raquel's hearing, and they were off riding again.

For her part, Raquel sat in silence to the rhythmic pulsing of horse hooves as she tried to untangle her thoughts.

Jake had been there last night. He'd been the one to unbind her hands and mouth, and Edom knew it too.

But *why*?

Her gaze skirted the trees, the mist, searching for what she felt so strongly was there. How Jake could keep pace, Raquel had no idea, but she felt his nearness even stronger now, after the night.

To what end?

The princes needed her blood to stop their curse—that much was clear—but why bother unbinding her? Edom had not bothered with her comfort; why had Jake?

I never lied, my bride. You simply refused to believe me.

Raquel continued searching the mist until, eventually, they drew upon a great fortress. Similar to the outpost, the mist stopped at its walls, but this was much larger. The moment they passed through the gate, a barren landscape spread before them, with rocky earth and rotting structures and a dried riverbed cutting it in half. The riverbed was like a royal carpet made of stones, spread out before the mouth of the fortress, and Raquel thought it had probably been beautiful once. With glittering blue water and vibrant green trees and a magnificent palace standing sentry over it all. But it was difficult to imagine that now with it so bathed in darkness and shadow, which Raquel found ironic for the Court of Light.

Edom led them through a small village of sorts as Forest kith emerged from buildings to see the source of commotion. He rode on for the castle without slowing until the road wound higher, over a bridge, and through the castle's wide-open doors.

Into a courtyard.

Prince Edom dismounted and pulled her down from the horse, then grabbed her by the rope as he dragged her after him toward the great doors in back.

Inside, the castle was like a great tomb. Candles stood everywhere, but their tiny flames could not chase away the shadow. Vines and tree roots had crept into the walls and ceiling like capillaries, cracking the stone in places. Raquel finally understood Jake's haste. She couldn't speak to the depravity he'd mentioned, but this castle could not physically stand much longer.

Nor could its king, apparently.

More Forest kith rushed to greet their prince, but Edom stormed on, pulling Raquel behind him, and it wasn't until they reached a quiet corridor that Edom stopped and addressed one of his men. "Lock her in the dungeon. I need to speak with my father first."

"Yes, Your Grace," the man said.

"And keep your eyes open for my brother," snarled the Bear Prince.

Rough hands grabbed her arms and shoved her on, away from the Bear Prince. They led her down a narrow stair that wound deeper and deeper into the earth, where cold seeped in and rot clung to the air.

Where bars designated the bowels of the castle.

One of the kith threw open a barred door. They shoved her inside and slammed the bars shut, and Raquel was left alone in the darkness.

20

Raquel did not know how long she sat in darkness. Time was a dream, a haze of cold and shadow, sometimes accented by the errant drip of water. She wrapped her arms around herself to keep warm, but the chill set deep in her bones.

Deep in her heart.

She'd been so certain that Jake had been following her, but now, locked in the belly of the fortress, that certainty fractured. How could he possibly rescue her now? And even if he managed to reappear, even if he managed to unlock her door and slip her out of this prison, how could they ever hope to escape?

Unless he didn't plan to rescue her.

Unless he didn't plan for her to leave this place alive.

He needs your blood. From your heart.

Raquel sank lower as disappointment weighed upon her shoulders, heavier and heavier, until she felt like collapsing beneath it all.

Edom was right. She was a fool.

And that foolishness had made her fail in her one objective: to save the people of Harran.

Perhaps I did save it, she thought bitterly. *Not because I succeeded in killing the forest prince, but because my blood will break the curse and Canna will no longer need brides from my people.*

However, this thought did not bring the joy Raquel had expected it to bring when she had set out on this mission. When she had been so ready to die for her cause.

She didn't feel so ready to die now.

Her dreams proved a torment, a constant banner of what could be, and Raquel found herself futilely clinging to them.

Mourning them.

Grieving them.

Hushed voices eventually sounded down the hall, where a golden glow appeared, dispelling the shadows, and three figures approached. One was undoubtedly the Bear Prince. His hulking silhouette was unmistakable.

He stopped before her bars, while his two kith stood behind him, and his black eyes glittered in the torchlight.

"Have you finally come to kill me?" Raquel said, weary.

A row of teeth shone within that full beard. "Not at this time, my bride. I have need of you yet." His voice had lost its wildness. It was softer now. More subdued.

"Get her out," he barked, and his two kith stepped forward. One unlocked the door, and the other strode inside, grabbed her arms, and hoisted her to her feet.

She was too weary to resist, too famished to pull away. Too heartbroken to fight.

The guards held her before their prince, who scrutinized her from head to toe, and then he abruptly turned and started down the hall. The guards dragged her after him, up the stairs and down more winding corridors through the palace while servants and guards alike gawked at her.

As though they had never before seen a mortal.

They eventually reached a set of engraved wooden doors, and Prince Edom made a fist and slammed it upon the wood so hard the door rattled upon its hinges.

"Enter!" said a thin male voice from within.

Edom pushed the door open, and the guards dragged Raquel after him.

Into a bedchamber.

It was a large space—large enough to hold her entire home in Harran—with arched ceilings and tall, narrow windows that probably would have illuminated this entire space with sunlight had the mist not obscured the world. Bookcases filled the walls, and luxurious furniture ornamented the floor. Raquel's gaze snagged upon a table trimmed in gold filigree that could have fed all of Harran for winter.

A cough rattled, and her attention slid to the enormous four-poster bed, where an old man lay.

King Issachar, Jake and Edom's father and the ruler of the Court of Light and all of Canna. It had to be. His hair was bushy, like Edom's, but shaded a midnight black like Jake's, though his was laced with silver. He had Edom's dark eyes, but his bore a milky sheen, and they did not focus, as if he could not quite see, but there was no mass to him. No muscle or strength. He was reed-thin, his frame hardly distinguishable from the thick blankets now covering him, and his skin was like paper, thin and wrinkled, and also sallow, and dark shadows pillowed his sunken eyes.

Jake had not lied about this much, at least.

Edom took two steps and knelt upon one knee, head bowed. He looked like a boulder with a mop for a head. "My king, I have brought the mortal," Edom said quietly, in that same subdued tone.

King Issachar's dark eyes slid from his son to Raquel, though still, they never focused. Not completely.

"Is it really you, my son?" King Issachar wheezed.

"Yes, Father. I would have returned sooner, but as you know, Jakobián took off with my bride. *Again*," Edom growled. "However, this time he planned to abscond with my birthright as well."

"How is that possible—"

"Mother glamoured him a coat, which he intended to use in order to receive your blessing."

The king lay quietly, and his next inhale rattled.

Edom lifted his head, and he looked pleadingly at the king. "Father, I beseech you: Please bestow the blessing that is mine by right so that this never happens again."

King Issachar stared at his eldest son and heir for so long Raquel wondered if he'd simply passed on. As if the news had been too much for him to endure, and so his soul had finally departed to find peace.

But then his eyelids slid closed, and a tremor rolled through his body. "Where is my Jakobián?" His voice was a pained whisper.

"Locked away with Mother, awaiting your punishment for their lies and treachery."

Raquel frowned. Edom's words were disconcerting, yes, but why were they having this conversation now? Hadn't Edom locked her away specifically so that he could speak with his father? Wouldn't they have already discussed this?

Or perhaps that was when Edom had intercepted Jake and locked him away.

Raquel's heart beat faster. She hated that she still cared.

"Then come near to me so that I may know you are my son Edom," King Issachar said.

"Of course, my king." Edom stood and strode forward, then stopped beside the bed and bowed his head.

The king reached out with a trembling hand and touched Edom's head. His fingers slid into that shaggy mass of hair, and relief smoothed his brow. Suddenly, an invisible force wrapped around Raquel like a blanket and jerked her forward so fast and so strong that Raquel nearly tripped on her own two feet. In fact, she would have, but the force had lifted her enough to drag her toes and hem across the black tiles to where it set her down next to Edom, beside the bed.

But that force did not let go.

Even so near death, King Issachar's power was astounding.

King Issachar reached out and pressed two fingers to Raquel's brow, and a shock of energy jolted through her body. Raquel would have collapsed if it weren't for the invisible vice still holding her upright.

"Let us hope she ends our curse once and for all," King Issachar said. Edom's head turned, and he glanced sideways at her while King Issachar closed his eyes.

"May the Fates give to you of heaven's due and earth's glory—an abundance of love and all the color absent from this world," King Issachar began. Where his voice had been quiet before, now it echoed with his power. Weaving promises into the continuum of time and space, across planes of possibility, and Raquel's entire body suddenly felt bathed in the sun's brilliant warmth, as if his words were knitting her into the tapestry of his new future.

"May this kingdom serve you," King Issachar continued, "and her people bow because of your just mercy, and may you lord over your kith and kin, and the sons of your kith bow before you. May those who curse you be cursed, and those who bless you be blessed."

With every word, that warmth bloomed hotter, brighter, until Raquel's entire being felt aflame.

This was the blessing Jake had spoken of. The one he'd needed so that the title of heir would pass on to him.

So that *he* could fulfill the curse.

And now he was too late, wherever he was. Edom had secured it from their father.

Her blood was his now.

Prince Edom reached out and placed his hand over his father's. "Thank you, Father. I will fulfill my duty to this kingdom." He turned his head and looked straight at Raquel, and his black eyes glittered. "And to my *beloved* bride."

Raquel stilled, gazing at him in confusion, but then the door burst open, and an enraged Prince Edom barreled through.

21

"*What have you done*?" this new Prince Edom roared. His eyes were wild, and one of them looked as though it was beginning to bruise.

The first Prince Edom, the one who had accepted King Issachar's blessing, stood suddenly, shoulders back and chest puffed out with victory. King Issachar looked utterly bewildered, glancing between the two Edoms, who were both spitting images of each other. But now that Raquel observed them together in the same room, she began to notice subtle differences. The variations that went beyond the physical, like the shining amusement in the eyes of the Edom beside her, and the subtle twist of his lips that looked very much like *Jake*.

Raquel didn't know how it was possible. She'd thought he needed his mother to mend the coat, but here he was, glamoured to look exactly like the real Prince Edom. Suddenly King Issachar's prior questions made sense. Edom had never made it to his father. Jake had intercepted him—somehow—momentarily disposed of him, and then come to Raquel's cell, glamoured as his brother.

Jake had stolen Edom's blessing and birthright after all.

"Well, well, well, how nice of you to join us," drawled the Edom beside her in Jake's smooth voice.

That was also why "Edom" had sounded different when he'd come to take her from her cell, Raquel realized. Because it had been *Jake* trying his best to match Edom's tone. He hadn't needed to do that when he'd come to Harran because those with him were already loyal to him.

And Prince Edom's face twisted with rage. "Tell me you did not bless him, Father!"

King Issachar's expression faltered, broken with understanding, and he sagged back upon his pillow as if the weight of this truth were too heavy to bear. "I did, my son, and he has received it. The binding is done."

Prince Edom—the real Prince Edom—stopped before them, looking caught between the desire to murder his brother and beg his father. "But surely you still have blessing left for me?"

"What else can I say?" King Issachar said with exasperation. "I made him lord over you and all your kith and kin, and I have exalted him with heaven's due and all the earth's glory." The king gazed upon his eldest, those milky eyes set with despair. "What else is left for you but to labor far away from your new master and future king?"

The real Prince Edom seethed, shoulders heaving, and his hands curled into fists at his sides as he glared at his brother.

There was a knock on the door.

All four of them glanced over as a guard burst through.

"Your Grace, Your Majesty..." He bowed quickly. "I am sorry to intrude, but there is—" His words trailed as he lifted his head and finally ingested the scene and the two Prince Edoms. The sight struck him mute, but a distant explosion brought him back.

It brought everyone back.

The only one who did not seem alarmed by the sound or shudder currently rolling through the floor was the Edom Imposter.

Jake.

He caught Raquel's gaze and winked as his father and the real Prince Edom both startled.

"What is happening?" King Issachar demanded, trying to shove himself to a seated position.

"That is why I came, sire," the guard continued. "We are under attack—"

"By whom?" roared the real Bear Prince.

"We can't be certain, Your Grace, but Gorva swears she saw Sienne in their ranks."

The real Edom cursed and ran to the window. "How many?"

"One thousand, Your Grace."

Edom's gaze whipped back in shock, King Issachar clutched his chest and slumped back upon his bed, and another explosion rocked the floor. Raquel wobbled unsteadily, but Jake caught her hand and didn't let go.

Their gazes met—held.

"*You*," the real Edom snarled.

Jake—still glamoured as his brother—released Raquel's hand and moved to stand between her and his furious brother.

The real Edom took a step even as the floor rocked with yet another explosion. "I will kill you for this," he snarled.

"No... wait..." King Issachar wheezed, his arm outstretched like a dying man reaching for what remained of his life.

And the real Edom charged his brother like a battering ram. They collided, both of them tumbling past Raquel, but then one Edom vanished. Just like that. If Raquel had blinked, she would have missed it, because he didn't stay invisible for long. The real Edom was just trying to regain his balance when Fake Edom appeared immediately behind him.

The real Edom growled in fury. "Cowardly little gnat. Stand before me and fight!"

Edom reached for him again, but Jake vanished and appeared behind him again, a wide smile upon his face. His sword of light winked into existence, and he smacked Edom across the back with the flat of it.

"Is that better?" the Fake Edom said in Jake's voice.

Edom whirled around like an enraged bear. "You're pathetic. You always have been. Gripping the backs of my heels to pull yourself ahead."

"You dare speak in such a manner to Canna's heir?" Jake's tone taunted.

Edom snarled and charged at Jake, but Jake vanished again. "Always running from the fight, just like when you were a sniveling little runt."

The Fake Edom reappeared, and he smiled wickedly. "A sniveling little runt that just stole your blessing."

Edom roared as he swung a massive fist, but the Fake Edom ducked away—or tried to. Edom caught the coat's hem at the last second, and he pulled.

Sliding the coat right off of Jake.

And then Jake was himself again.

"There you are, little brother," Edom spat, and he ripped the coat in two.

King Issachar cried out.

Jake glanced over as the king's head rolled to the side, his milky eyes blank as they stared at the ceiling.

"Father!" Jake yelled and started for him, but Edom's gaze settled on Raquel.

And Raquel ran.

She'd made it two steps before Edom grabbed her skirts and jerked her back. Raquel gasped in surprise, then slipped the blade from her corset, turned, and tried to plunge it into his chest, but he grabbed her wrist and wrenched it from her fingers, not caring that the metal cut his skin. Not caring that he bled.

He jerked her around and pressed the blade to her throat. "Enough!"

Jake stopped two paces away from them. His eyes were dark, his expression lethal as he stared at Edom, at the knife against Raquel's throat. "Let her go, Edom. Your quarrel is with me."

"Which is precisely why I cannot let her go," Edom said. "She is the only way I can get your attention."

Raquel's heart leapt at Edom's little insinuation. Which was utterly ridiculous, considering he had a knife at her throat. But Jake didn't deny it either, and that hope burned brighter.

"Another step and she dies," Edom said.

"You wouldn't."

"I would."

"You know we need this."

"*You* need this. I have no use for her. You stole my birthright, traitorous worm."

Jake's expression darkened, his body tensing. "You would destroy this kingdom and everything in it."

Edom looked long at Jake. "And you would be the king of nothing."

Raquel sensed Edom's move the split second before it happened. Like a dream playing in slow motion, she watched, knowing what was coming but unable to move fast enough to stop it. She watched him pull back the knife, watched it arc down toward her chest. waiting and knowing it would cut right through her heart and spill her blood all over the tiles so that Jake could never use it.

So that Jake could never heal this land from its curse.

She tried to slip away, but she couldn't move fast enough. The blade gleamed as it arched down, and down, and—

Jake appeared right in front of her, shoved her away, and the knife plunged into his chest instead.

22

Raquel gasped as Jake's body absorbed the impact, and he stumbled back into her.

"You fool!" Edom crowed as he laughed.

Jake's weight was too much for Raquel, and she collapsed beneath him just as something exploded through the window.

Giant wings flapped, and a horrible shriek echoed.

A Depraved.

What in the... what was a Depraved doing here? *Now*? Raquel's attention was torn between this new horror and the man currently bleeding to death on top of her.

The Depraved landed on the floor, its wings arched behind it like some avenging demon, and Raquel's eyes widened as she realized she knew it.

This was the Depraved from the forest. The smaller one that had stopped and looked at her as if...

It had recognized her.

And it was looking at her now.

Familiarity pricked at Raquel—something that went beyond the physical. It shone in the soul trapped behind those glassy black eyes, and a chill swept over Raquel, head to toe. She remembered something Jake had said about the mist, the curse.

It comes to claim all of us eventually.

Jake had not lied. Adina *had* been alive when he'd last seen her. He just failed to mention he'd lost her to the curse.

"Adina…?" Raquel's voice fell out at a whisper.

In answer, the small Depraved tipped its head and squawked like a bird of prey.

Which Edom seized as opportunity, sword in hand.

"Adina, lookout!"

The Depraved looked over just as Edom nearly made contact, then flapped its wings and pushed off the ground. Edom's sword sliced through air, but before he could regain balance, the Depraved grabbed hold of the back of his shirt and lifted him.

Edom screamed and yelled and kicked and swung, but the Depraved did not let go. It hovered there near the ceiling as it looked at Raquel and cocked its head, and then it soared out through the window it had already broken with a howling Edom in its clutches.

And then the castle trembled violently.

Raquel fell over Jake and covered him with her body as best she could until the trembling stopped, and then she finally looked at him, at his injury.

At the blade sticking out of his chest, where blood bloomed bright and cruel.

"I…told you she still lived." Jake tried to smile, but then he coughed. Blood stained his lips and splattered his chest.

"You idiot! Why did you sacrifice your life for me?" Raquel yelled at him, though she already knew the reason. The only reason anyone ever sacrificed their life for another. "I thought you didn't—"

Jake gripped her hand so tight. "I…saw them too."

Raquel blinked blurry eyes. "What? Saw what? What are you talking about—"

"We named the boy Ronan. And the girl Adi, after your mother, and she"—he coughed more blood, and Raquel felt as if that blade were suddenly in *her* chest—"looked exactly like you." Jake lifted a hand and placed it upon her cheek, and Raquel choked on her tears. "So...beautiful."

Raquel laid her hand over Jake's. "*Why are you telling me this now*?" She was so angry at him. "Tell me how to help you! There has to be something...some form of magik—"

The floor trembled again, and more bits of rock rained down. Raquel tried to cover Jake's body, but he grabbed her hand and held it to his chest, beside the knife, where his tunic was soaked in blood.

And he looked at her.

His eyes were molten but dimming before her eyes. "It was never your heart I needed to claim. It was mine. And you did." His expression relaxed, his hand slipped, and the light faded completely.

"No..." Raquel shook him, again and again. "No!" Raquel screamed as more rock fell all around them. "We have a little house in the woods, and a child on the way, and you..." But the light was gone. His honeyed eyes dulled and stared at nothing.

Raquel's chest twisted in anguish, and she fell over him, sobbing. Not really sure why it hurt so much, only that it did, and she found it suddenly very difficult to breathe. "You told me you loved me, and I...I never got the chance to say it back."

Everything stopped. The trembling, the sound. Everything. The world was quiet, and then a bird chirped a fluttering melody nearby, and Raquel opened her eyes to...color.

Bright and brilliant.

A warm sun flickered through the treetops and mottled the forest floor in golden light.

At first she wondered if the curse had broken. If the disease and rot had vanished and returned this kingdom to its former glory, except the details caught up to her fast. When she'd closed her eyes, she'd been in the palace, but she was no longer in that palace. She was in a densely wooded forest. One she knew well, for it was just outside of Harran.

Jake lay on the ground before her, his eyes closed as though he were merely asleep, but that couldn't be...

Wait.

Raquel stilled.

There was no knife, no signs of any injury. No blood stained his tunic.

"Impossible..." she whispered. Frantic, and a little hopeful, she pulled at the ties of his tunic and opened the front so that she could see where the blade had sunk into his chest.

And then his hands wrapped firmly around her wrists, stopping her.

Raquel's gaze met his bright golds, which shimmered like the thread of the coat his mother had enchanted. A coat he was *wearing*. How was that possible? She'd watched Edom tear it in half! But there it was, sure as the sun, and it was no longer brown but the warm honey of his eyes, and when he shifted, the fabric reflected light and all its colors, like a prism. As if the coat had trapped light and color inside of itself.

"How... the knife...?" she stuttered, but then Jake released her hands and shoved himself to a seated position. He looked down at himself and touched his chest where the knife had been, and his brow wrinkled with confusion and wonder. His gaze shot to the trees, the high branches and blue sky and the sun shining brilliantly beyond.

And then he closed his eyes.

For a long moment, he didn't move—didn't seem to breathe. He simply sat there, his face turned toward the sun as a light breeze ruffled his hair, and Raquel couldn't look away from him. There was color to his skin that had not been there before, a flush to his cheeks that made him even more striking—how that was possible, Raquel didn't know.

And then those eyes snapped open and landed on her with such force, it knocked the breath from her lungs.

"You saved me," he said so softly.

Raquel was speechless, trapped in his gaze, her heart feeling suddenly too large for her chest. Especially as he reached out with one hand, cupped her cheek, and threaded his fingers into her hair, gazing at her in the way that Dream Jake would have done.

"The heart I needed to claim was never yours. It was a mortal heart I needed to claim...for myself," he said, putting the pieces together for both of them.

"So you are mortal now," Raquel managed, struggling to follow but also entirely distracted by the warmth of his palm upon her cheek.

He pulled away to grab her hand instead, then pressed her palm to his bare chest, where his heart beat a strong and steady rhythm. "As mortal as they come, my bride."

Raquel was caught somewhere between overwhelming joy and fear for him. "But what about your magik? How will you ever survive in your own kingdom?"

He glanced past her, at the trees above. "I do not think I am going back to Canna." A beat passed, and his brow furrowed. "I do not...feel the veil anymore."

"Does that mean the curse is broken?"

An errant breeze stirred his hair. "I do not know."

"But what about Sienne, and the children—"

He squeezed her hand firmly, and he looked back at her. "Whatever has come of Canna's curse, Sienne is strong, and she will do her best to help our people endure."

Because King Issachar was gone. "I'm so sorry about your father," she said.

Jake inhaled deeply as his thumb traced little circles inside her palm. "I am too, but he is finally at peace now. And my mother...well, she has always been adept at taking care of herself. Wherever she is."

"She did not mend your coat?"

Jake shook his head. "*I* did. I found the thread while we were searching her private residence, and mended the coat while I followed you and Edom to the palace. Though nothing I did made it appear like...*this*."

They sat quietly, gazing upon this wondrous and iridescent fabric while his thumb continued tracing circles on her palm.

"You knew about Adina," Raquel said at last.

"I stole her from Edom and hid her away at my mother's in hopes of winning her affections, but she escaped into the forest and intercepted the Depraved." He stopped tracing circles and looked at her. "Given how much you cared for her, I thought it a cruel thing to share."

"I was right," she whispered, and Jake arched a brow. "You did have a heart all along."

His lips curled, that familiar mischief lit his eyes, and he released her hand to hold her chin instead.

Raquel stilled, held captive by his touch, and her heart drummed so hard and so fast, she thought it might beat right out of her chest.

"It seems you were right about me all along," he said lowly, then leaned in close, his eyes hooded as his warm breath feathered across her lips. "You also mentioned we had a house in these woods."

Raquel felt suddenly hot all over. "You heard that?"

His lips brushed hers. Teasing, taunting. "And I believe you were going to tell me you loved me back."

Raquel pulled back an inch, bewildered that he had heard any of it, but then he smiled that mischievous smile she so loved, pulled her in, and kissed her mouth once. Twice. Just a touch, but not nearly enough, and yet it still sent shivers through her body.

"You've haunted me every moment of every day since I first laid eyes upon you," he whispered upon her lips. "I figured I might as well let you have me and be done with it to end my misery."

Raquel smiled. "Let *me* have *you*—?"

Jake flipped her onto her back and positioned himself over her. He rested his weight upon his elbows, his hips upon hers. His face was a handsbreadth away, and his eyes were huge and dark as they bored into hers. "I had never known love, until I saw pieces of it in my dreams. Of you." He brushed the hair back from her face, so tenderly. "My beloved bride." His finger trailed her lips, and it took everything in her not to pull his lips down to hers right then, but he was not finished speaking. "You were right. Love is far more valuable than living, and so I traded my immortality for a heart." His thumb pressed into her bottom lip, his gaze burned into hers, and suddenly she understood what he'd been trying to tell her about the curse. About his needing to claim a heart.

How that was the only thing that could heal their rotting kingdom.

"And I will love you with all of it for the rest of my numbered days," he continued. "And I will love our children, and their children, until I have no days left, but I've realized there is no death when one loves, for love is its own sort of immortality."

Raquel smiled up at him as she wrapped her arms around his neck and played with a clump of his silky black hair. "I am relieved to hear you finally speaking sense."

Jake smirked and slowly lowered his mouth to her neck, where he planted one soft kiss. Then another. Each touch was a little flame to her skin, and Raquel closed her eyes, reveling in his warmth and the solid weight of his body. Wanting *more*. She slid her hand down his back, feeling the muscles shift and flex, and his breath shuddered.

"You also mentioned we had a child on the way..." he murmured against her skin, and his fingertips danced over the ribs of her corset.

Raquel's heart skipped a beat. "A third. Yes."

"Then we had better get started, because, as you said, my days are now numbered."

Raquel laughed, Jake smiled like the sun, and he kissed her deeply.

EPILOGUE

Deep in the woods, there stood a little house. And at this house lived a little family: a father, a mother, and their three children. Two boys and one girl. Most would call them poor, for they did not possess much in the way of material things, and what they did own bore the scars of age and ample use. But they understood—as very few understand—that it is not *things* that make one rich.

It is love and the relationships rooted within it.

And *that*, they had in abundance.

They could have sold the coat. That gleaming gold anomaly from another place, from another time. It would have earned them a treasure of coin, this artifact from the other side of the veil. But the father knew well what gold did to a man and what greed did to a kingdom, and they held fast to this symbol of what had been, of what they had overcome.

So that they would never be tempted into depravity again.

And so one night, while the children were asleep, after Jake had told them the story of the coat for the hundredth time and he saw how that golden hue gleamed in his eldest's eyes, he and his beloved bride neatly folded it up, wrapped it in cloth, and buried it deep in the earth. They tried to destroy it first—tried to throw it in fire—but this coat was from another world, and it could not be harmed by this one.

As Jake dumped the last bit of dirt over the buried treasure with his shovel, Raquel slipped her fingers through his and rested her head against his shoulder.

"It won't stay buried forever," she said. "The truth never does."

"Then let it stay buried for now," he replied as he squeezed her hand gently. "Until the world is ready to receive it."

THE END...

....for now.

About the Series

Arranged Marriages of the Fae is a multi-author series of short novels written by seven romantic fantasy authors on the same theme. These books can be read on their own, but you'll have so much more fun if you read the whole series!

As authors, we want to thank you for getting swept away by our fantasy romances and we wish you hours of enjoyment and escape!

Married by Wind
Married by Fate
Married by Scandal
Married by War
Married by Treachery
Married by Starfall
Married by Dusk

www.arrangedmarriagesofthefae.com

ALSO BY BARBARA KLOSS

THE GODS OF MEN SERIES

The Gods of Men

Temple of Sand

A Symphony of Stars

THE PANDORAN NOVELS

Gaia's Secret

The Keeper's Flame

Breath of Dragons

Heir of Pendel

ABOUT THE AUTHOR

Barbara studied biochemistry at Cal Poly, San Luis Obispo, CA, and worked for years as a clinical laboratory scientist. She was lured there by mental images of colorful bubbling liquids in glass beakers. She was deceived. Always an avid reader, especially of fantasy, she began drafting her own stories, writing worlds and characters that were never beyond saving.

She currently lives in northern California with her gorgeous husband, three kids, and pup. When she's not writing, she's usually reading, trekking through the wilderness, playing the piano, or gaming—though she doesn't consider herself a gamer. She just happens to like video games. RPGs, specifically. Though now that her kids are getting older, she's finding she has to share her gaming consoles more than she would like.

www.barbarakloss.com
contact@barbarakloss.com

Be sure to sign up for Barbara's email newsletter:
https://www.subscribepage.com/barbarakloss

facebook.com/GaiasSecret
instagram.com/barbaraklossbooks
amazon.com/~/e/B005V06A0I

www.ingramcontent.com/pod-product-compliance
Lightning Source LLC
Chambersburg PA
CBHW070549310726
48982CB00011B/1515/J
* 9 7 8 1 7 3 4 4 5 7 3 9 1 *